Printed in Great Britain
by Amazon

Relentless

Christopher Artinian

CHRISTOPHER ARTINIAN

ISBN: 9798642201046

DEDICATION

To the kindness of strangers.

ACKNOWLEDGEMENTS

Thank you to my amazing wife, Tina, who never lets me down, and is always there for me.

A huge thank you to the gang across in the fan club on Facebook. A nicer and more supportive bunch of people I could never wish to meet.

Thank you to my good friend, Christian Bentulan, for another incredible cover. Also, many thanks to my editor, Ken.

And finally, a very big thank you to you for purchasing this book.

1

Sal opened her eyes. The sun was just peeking through the bright green canopy, and the sounds and smells of the forest enveloped her. Despite the fogginess, two thoughts immediately entered her head. *How the hell did I get here? And where on earth is here, exactly?*

She sat up slowly and looked around. The ground was littered with twigs and leaves. The small clearing she was in was surrounded by dense woodland in every direction. She climbed to her feet, brushing off the remains of the forest floor detritus that had attached itself to her. The last thing she remembered was getting ready to go out with her best friend, Lauren. They were going to enjoy a nice meal and a quiet drink together before the full-on no-holds-barred circus that would be her hen night the following evening.

Wait a minute, no, that wasn't the last thing she remembered. It was coming back to her now. They had gone to Fabio's in town, just next to the railway station. They'd had a couple of drinks there then they bumped into their friends, Pippa, Amber and Suzie, and then... Then what? Why was everything so hazy? Why couldn't she remember? *Oh my God, I've turned into my druggie, alky mother, waking up God knows where with God knows who.*

Wait a minute. What an idiot. This is the start of it. This is some kind of prank. The girls must have slipped me a roofie, driven me out here, and any minute the hen party is going to start.

Sal studied her surroundings. Part of her was furious that they'd even think about doing this; part of her was amused and excited that they would go to such lengths to pull off something she would never, ever forget.

She glanced down to see she was wearing the same casual attire as she had been for her night out—T-shirt, jeans, Doc Martens. She checked her pockets and giggled to herself. She had been running late the previous evening. Dan, her fiancé, had bought her a key fob personal alarm and torch—*he was so protective.* She had intended to remove it before going out because the chances were good that she would set it off accidentally when she was pissed and wake up the entire block of flats. But there it was.

She looked around where she had been lying, but there was no sign of her handbag. *Hopefully, Lauren will keep it safe for me.* It was warm for the time of year, and the midges were starting to rise into the air. "Okay, you lot," she shouted, "you got me. This beats the time we tied Amber to a chair and left her in the middle of that roundabout. I can't wait to see what else you've got planned, but whatever it is, you need to hurry up 'cause these bitey little fuckers are really starting to get on my baps."

Sal twirled around peering through the woodland, waiting for one or all of her friends to appear, but for several minutes all she could see was trees. Then she caught movement out of the corner of her eye. She turned and squinted, smiling a little at the same time. *Is that Lauren? No, too tall to be Lauren. Carrie perhaps?* She continued watching as the figure tore towards her, hurdling over bushes and ducking beneath low-hanging branches with athletic prowess. *Who the hell is this?*

The figure burst from the shadows and into the

clearing. Sal stood glued to the spot. Her mouth dropped open. It was a woman … a stranger; she held a sharp stone in her fist. Blood coated the back of her hand and face and stained her otherwise beige vest.

The woman's hand shot out and grabbed Sal's upper arm in a vice-like grip.

"RUUUN!"

2

The stranger pulled Sal hard, forcing her to move, which she did. *Is this real? Is this part of a game?*

Whatever it was, the adrenaline was surging through her as she followed the other woman at breakneck speed through the forest. She leapt where the stranger leapt, ducked where the stranger ducked. After two minutes running flat out, Sal shouted, "Stop! I need to stop."

She bent over double, resting her hands on her thighs and desperately trying to catch her breath. "We can't. Not yet," the stranger replied, taking hold of Sal's arm and starting to drag her once again.

Sal struggled loose. "Stop it. This isn't funny. I need to catch my breath."

"Funny? Funny? I'm trying to save your life."

"Yeah … sure …" Sal replied in between laboured breaths. "Where's Lauren?"

The stranger looked confused. "I don't know who you're talking about."

"Oh, you're good. So, what is this? Are you an actress? Is this some role-playing game? Or are you a friend of one of the others?"

The other woman's brow creased for a second. "Look, I don't know what you think's going on, but this is no game. I've not heard of this Lauren. I don't know who the fuck you are. All I know is that I've seen six of my friends caught by these sick bastards in the last twenty-four hours and I'm damned sure I'm not going to let the same thing happen to me. Now stay here or come with me, I really don't give a fuck."

The stranger started running again, leaving Sal just standing there, bewildered. She glanced around. On a good day, she would have struggled to retrace her steps to where she had woken up. Today was not a good day. She turned to see the stranger weaving in and out of the trees, a few more seconds and she would probably lose sight of her for good.

"Wait. Wait for me," Sal screamed and started sprinting after her.

At first, the stranger didn't slow down, she merely glimpsed back, but eventually she steadied her pace then stopped until Sal caught up.

"Listen, another five minutes or so, and then we can rest for a bit. I know a place that's a bit safer than out here."

"Where are we? What is this?" Part of Sal wanted this to be a game, a hen night prank, but the more she saw what lingered behind the stranger's eyes, the more she began to believe this was real.

"When we stop, I'll tell you what I know, but right now, we need to keep going, and for God's sake, keep your eyes peeled."

"For what?"

"For anything. Nothing here is what it seems."

3

Lauren slowly roused. Her eyes scratched open, and she just sat there for a moment trying to remember any possible reason why she would be waking up leant against a tree in what looked like a big forest. She stared down at her bare legs. She remembered how pissed off she had been that Sal had underdressed for their night on the town, and now she'd give anything to be wearing a pair of Levi's and some comfortable trainers instead of the little black dress and stilettos that she was fashioning.

She slapped her thigh hard as a buzzy thing with big wings landed on her. *What the hell is going on?*

She climbed to her feet, a little unsteady at first. She used the trunk of the sturdy tree to give her balance until she was totally upright. "Hello … Sal … you there?" she called, but all she heard in reply were the sounds of the forest and her own words echoing back at her. Her bare arms and legs prickled as uncertainty quickly turned to fear. She didn't remember much of the previous evening. There had been a number of occasions when she'd woken up not remembering much from the night before, but it had always been in a bed, never like this. "Sal? Hello?"

She started walking and, after just a few seconds, came to a halt. The uneven ground was not a good match for the high heels. She slipped them off and suddenly turned back towards the tree where she had awoken. Her handbag … the petite Gucci wallet that she'd blown half a month's pay on … her phone … her life was inside that bag. *Dammit, I've been robbed and dumped out here.*

Where was Sal? *Oh my God, I hope she's okay.* She started walking again. The earth was cool beneath her feet, despite the warmth of the surrounding air. The canopy of the trees protected much of it from the direct sunlight. She stopped again suddenly, and even her goose bumps got goose bumps. In the space of a few seconds, the forest around her had fallen silent, almost as if it had been sucked into a giant vacuum. Lauren's heart began to pound in her chest.

The atmosphere was electric, heightening her anxiety. Maybe her robber hadn't just dumped her. Maybe he had brought her here with something else in mind and been watching her as she slept waiting to have a little fun when she woke up. She swallowed hard as a sheen of nervous sweat made her dress cling to her. Eyes were on her … she could feel them. Somebody was studying her, observing her. Any second, they would jump out and reveal their intentions.

Lauren turned full circle. They could be anywhere, hidden behind any tree. Then another thought occurred to her and she looked up. Who was to say they were behind a tree? Hell, they could be in a tree, ready to just drop down in front of her.

The sound of her beating heart became deafening, blocking out everything else, blocking out the capacity to reason, the possibility for rational thought.

But then, just as quickly, she became deaf to it. It was replaced by a whisper in the back of her mind. The whisper gradually grew in volume until it thundered in her head.

Run, run, run, run, RUN, RUN, RUUUN!

4

"Help me! Please, someone, help me!" The terrified scream rang through the forest, bouncing off the trees, and it took Lauren a few seconds to get a bearing on where it had come from. She stopped running.

"Hello?" she called.

"Hello? Hello! Please help me."

"Pip? Pip, is that you?"

"Lauren?"

"Where are you?"

"I'm in some kind of a pit."

"What?"

Pip started sobbing. "I don't know what's going on."

"Okay. Okay. Just keep calling out, I'll find you."

Lauren looked around. She had not forgotten that weird feeling that someone was watching her, but there was no way she could abandon a friend in need.

"I don't know what's happening. I woke up about five minutes ago, and I was in this hole. I don't know what's going on," she cried out before starting to sob once again like a frightened child.

"It's okay. It's okay, Pip. Don't worry, we'll get you out of there."

"And there's blood. Lots of blood. I think it's some kind of animal trap or something."

"I'm coming, Pip. I'm coming."

"I don't remember anything. I don't remember how I got here."

"Yeah, join the club. I woke up a few minutes ago myself, and I don't have a clue."

"Oh my God! Oh my God! There's—"

"What? What is it?"

Suddenly, Lauren's voice was much closer. "Here. I'm here. Please hurry. I'm scared, Lauren. I'm scared."

Lauren came to a halt as the ground opened up in front of her. There was no warning, no lip, no curb, just a hole about six feet wide, seven feet long and ten feet deep. Pip stared up at her with wide, teary eyes. Shuddering breaths left the back of her friend's throat as she held up what looked like a Pandora bracelet.

"What is it?"

"What does it look like, Lauren?"

"It looks like a charm bracelet."

"Yeah … and it's not mine."

"So?"

"The blood on these walls … I don't think it's animal blood."

5

A shiver ran down Lauren's back. She had known there was something very wrong about this entire situation from the moment she had woken up, but now she realised this was all part of something bigger. The pit that Pippa was trapped in was tiled. It had been carefully dug out of the ground, out here in the middle of nowhere, and someone had gone to the trouble of lining it and tiling it. On the far wall at floor level, there was a one-foot vertical metal grate. What purpose that served she had no clue. She looked at the bloodstains decorating the walls and then noticed something else. She knelt down and reached in, sliding her right index finger over the surface of a tile. She looked at it, rubbed her fingers together and brought them up to her nose.

"What? What is it?" Pippa asked in between sobs.

"I … I think it's lard."

"Wh—what?"

"Somebody has covered the walls in lard."

"Why? Why would they do that?"

"Why would someone have this hole out here in the first place? None of this makes sense, Pip, I just know we need to get you out of there." Lauren turned to look around.

"Don't leave me."

"I need to find something to help you climb out."

"I'm scared."

"I know, Pip. I am too. Just give me a minute, and I'll be back."

Lauren disappeared, leaving her friend alone in the blood-painted cell. Pip dabbed her eyes with the back of her hands, in turn wiping them on her jeans. *What the hell is going on here?* She desperately tried to bring her breathing under control. Crying wasn't going to get her out of this. "Don't go too far," she called.

"Don't worry. I'm not going to leave you."

Pip looked up through the branches and trees to the bright blue sky. Soon she would be out of this hole and together with her friend they could try to understand what was going on. She took a step nearer to the wall to examine it more closely when her foot dipped. For a second, she thought it was a loose tile, but then a metallic clunk made her spin around, and she saw the narrow metal grate on the far wall sink into the ground. She looked down and saw the tile she had stepped on slowly shifting back into position. It was some kind of mechanical release. Pip tilted her head like a curious dog. Another clunk, virtually a muted echo came from further within the dark recesses of the grate, and then a third and a fourth. *What the hell?*

She got down onto her hands and knees, angling her head as close to the tiled floor as she could get without actually putting her face to the bloody surface. All she could see was darkness beyond darkness, but now there was a draught, a warm breeze carrying a thick putrid stench towards her. She curled her nose and stifled the urge to retch, but then something besides the smell made her feel sick to her stomach—a sound. No, not one sound, a whole chorus of sounds. The drumming of hundreds of tiny pattering feet punctuated only by the odd excited squeak and screech.

Pip sprang back to her feet; her entire body was shaking. "Lauren! Lauren! LAUREN!"

Her friend came running back to the hole, she had found a branch, and there was a look of irritation on her face. "I told you I was just—"

A moving carpet of foul-smelling terror flooded through the gap where the grate had been just moments before. For a split second, both girls froze in utter horror as the brown furry bodies jostled and fought for position.

Lauren looked down into her friend's terrified, tear-filled eyes. "Lauren … help me," Pip whispered.

6

The stranger stuck her left hand out, bringing Sal to an immediate stop. "What?"

"Shh," the stranger replied, pulling them both behind the cover of a tree. "Up ahead," she whispered then looked down to the ground. She grabbed a fist-sized rock and handed it to Sal.

"What's this for?"

"You'll know when you need it."

The pair edged forward slowly; then Sal saw them as well. Two figures standing in the shadows beneath a colossal oak tree. The tension in the air was palpable, and Sal felt her grip involuntarily tighten around the rock in her hand. She understood now, she knew what the stone was for.

The two women crouched as they moved, zigging and zagging between the trees. *This is crazy. I have no idea what's going on, I have no idea who this woman I'm with is, but we're about to attack a couple of people I've never even laid eyes on before.*

They carried on moving, speeding up with each step they took, afraid at any minute they could be spotted before the attack. Thirty metres.

The stranger tapped Sal on the arm and signalled for them to split up—a two-pronged assault. Twenty metres—the shadows beneath the tree started moving away. *This should make it easier.*

Ten metres—*I know that pink hair.* "Suzie!" Sal shouted.

The two figures stopped and turned, and the stranger came to a skidding halt too, the dagger-like stone in her blood-covered hand already raised in attack position.

"Aagghh!" It was Amber who let out a stifled scream as the wild-eyed woman loomed just a few feet from her.

"Jesus!" the stranger said, letting out a relieved

breath. "Sorry. Thought you were them."

Suzie looked at the stranger then ran towards Sal. They threw their arms around each other; then Amber did the same. When their embraces finally broke, the friends pulled back to look at one another.

"What the hell's going on?" Suzie and Amber asked at exactly the same time.

"I just woke up here a few minutes ago, I thought it was something you guys had planned for the hen party."

"Ha! Trust me, unless a male stripper dressed as a fireman jumps out from behind one of these trees and dangles his plum sack in your face, absolutely none of this was to do with us," Suzie replied.

"Who's your friend?" Amber asked.

"I don't know," Sal replied, and all three of them looked towards the young woman in the bloodstained vest.

"My name's Gabby."

"So, do you think you can tell us what the hell's going on here now?" Sal asked.

"Soon. We're not far away from—"

A shriek cut through the forest like a machete and panic seized all four women.

"Lauren, HELP ME!"

"That's Pip. Come on," Sal said and started sprinting in the direction the scream had risen from.

7

There was a part of Lauren that wanted to scream at the top of her voice. There was another part that wanted to run and keep on running, but she knew she was Pip's only hope. She lowered the long branch down into the pit; the first of the rats were mere inches away from Pip as she grasped on to the sturdy bough like her life depended on it, which, of course, it did.

Pip placed a foot on the wall, hoping the branch would give her enough purchase despite the greased surface, but it was not to be. Her foot slammed back down, and the pained squeal of one of the rats sent a tremor of fear through her. She looked down in horror to see her feet covered and the rats climbing over one another in order to get to her.

"Aaarrrggghhh!" She let go of the branch and frantically jumped, shuddered and swept, desperate to free herself from the snapping, clawing battalions of flesh-hungry vermin that were still emerging from the gap where the grate had been. "Help me, help me, Lauren," she cried desperately, like an infant, as razor-sharp teeth tore through her thick denim jeans. "Aeooowww!" another howl of pain erupted from her lungs as the rats continued to scale her body, latching on to anything they could—ankles, calf muscles, thighs. They battled one another, desperate to find a fresh piece of meat where they could sink their incisors.

Lauren was crying too now. She thrust the branch further into the pit. "Take it! Take it, Pip!"

Pip seized it with everything she had and closed her eyes. The acute pain was secondary to the terrifying realisation that she was moments away from being stripped to the bone unless a miracle happened. She wasn't sure, but she thought she lost control of her bladder as her friend began to hoist her up once more. She felt warm damp patches all over her body as cloth and skin was torn in a rapid flurry of snapping heads.

"Make it stop. Make it stop," she wept as Lauren pulled harder than ever. Pip's body, little by little, began to rise off the ground. Her left side pushed against the greased wall, trapping some of the feeding creatures momentarily before they let go, losing their prime position and falling back into the manic, scrambling throng. The flexible bough continued to move upwards as Lauren let out loud grunts of exertion.

Pip held on even tighter, and with each heave a few

more of the filthy, disease-ridden creatures fell. Others leapt at her, the odd one managed to grasp on, but for the first time there was a tiny bit of hope. In body at least, Lauren was a strong woman. She went jogging every day, she played league softball, if she could carry on, Pip could get out of this. She looked down to see dozens of rats desperately trying to run up the greased walls but to no avail. It was working. This was it; she was going to get out.

Suddenly, Pip felt something tugging on her left breast. She looked down to see the filthy rodent's hungry black eyes staring up at her. The creature was about the size of a small cat, and it peeled back its lips revealing blood-covered teeth. Pip felt sure that any second it would pounce at her face. She closed her eyes; she couldn't take any more. Then it came. She felt the talon-like claws sink into her cheeks, she did not cry out though; the only fear she had bigger than this was that one of these monstrous things would leap into her open mouth. Inside, however, she screamed a thousand screams. They were loud enough to deafen the gods. She waited, fully expecting the giant rat's teeth to begin ripping at her any second, but the attack never came.

She dared to snatch a glance, but the rat had disappeared. Despite everything else that was happening, her heart lifted a little. *It must have fallen off*. She was still inching higher and higher, thanks to Lauren, and any moment she would be out of this pit, then together they could batter away any hangers-on. Of course, when they finally broke free of this nightmare, she would need shots. Yes, a hell of a lot of shots, but whereas a few seconds ago she was convinced it was all over, now there was some possibility of light at the end of the tunnel. Even the shifting, clawing, biting filth that was still attached to her seemed a little less terrifying as the possibility of escape loomed ever nearer.

8

Lauren hated rats … hated them. She knew it was an irrational fear; she had suffered with it ever since childhood, but it was a fear nonetheless and, given the current situation, not one she could easily avoid. She also knew that the only thing standing between Pip and a gruesome, painful demise was her strength and determination.

All those self-help and inner strength seminars, all those trips to the gym, all that private training, all the morning swims … all forgotten as a giant rat pounced from her friend's cheek onto the thick bough and lunged towards Lauren.

Like some crazed, furry, flesh-craving missile, it flew towards her face. It was instinct, a need to self-preserve, that made Lauren let go of the branch and throw her arms up. In that split second, her heart died a little as the realisation that she had just killed her friend consumed her.

***

Shock, disbelief, horror, despair and a multitude of other feelings and emotions shrouded Pip as, suddenly, she and the branch plummeted into the pit. She fell backwards smashing her head against the tiled wall. It was just seconds later that she lost sight of the blue sky as a hundred filth-encrusted warm furry bodies engulfed her.

She couldn't help it, she screamed. She screamed a panic-stricken, wide-mouthed scream to the heavens, and her worst nightmare came true. A fat, brittle-furred creature lunged into her mouth. The increased volume of her howl had no bearing on its intrepid exploration as she felt its claws tense and tear into her tongue.

If she had a thousand nightmares a night for a thousand years, not one of them could match this.

***

Lauren fell backwards as she felt the giant rodent make contact with her arm. It tried to sink its claws in but failed, and as she hit the earth, the creature flew above her. *Need to get to my feet now!*

She sprang back up and braced herself for the vile thing's next attack. She did not have to wait long. It landed on the earth, rolled and tore back towards her. *All those times people said, 'They're more scared of you than you are of them'—what total bullshit!*

It didn't leap this time, it just continued running, right along the floor and straight up her bare leg. She was deaf to the muffled scream and excited squeals from the pit behind her as the furry brown demon ran up her short dress. Lauren was frozen in fear watching it happen; to bat it off she would need to touch it, she would need to put her hands in range of those razor-sharp teeth.

"Lauren! Lauren!" it was a call from a familiar voice, but she was transfixed, mesmerised, petrified. All she could concentrate on, all she could see was this thing radiating malevolence that was tearing towards her face like a guided missile.

***

All the bites and scratches, all the pain and tears, it meant nothing now. This was how Pip was going to die, choking on a fat, smelly ball of vileness as it tore and clawed at her tongue and the back of her throat. She retched and vomited, but the rat was wedged like a cork. Pip's body convulsed as she desperately gasped and writhed for air, but it was too late. It was all too late. In a teary judder of agony, Pip closed her eyes forever.

9

It was like a magician's trick—now you see it, now you don't. The rat vanished. It took Lauren's brain a few seconds to catch up with current events, but then she heard that familiar voice again.

"Lauren … Lauren." It was Sal. Even through her tear-filled eyes, she could see it was her friend.

The rat was being held by a woman she didn't recognise. It squirmed and struggled in her hand, desperate to free itself, but the woman merely flung it back down into the pit to join the rest of the thrashing brown bodies.

Lauren burst out crying as she watched. "Pip's down there. I killed her. She was depending on me, and I killed her."

Sal pulled her friend away from the edge of the hole and held her tightly. "It's okay, Lauren. It's okay."

Lauren pulled back, "No, it's not," she screamed. "I killed her. I killed Pip. I let her die to save myself because I'm a pathetic fucking coward."

"That's not true." It was Amber's turn to try to comfort her now. Her friends were devastated for Lauren and Pip. Inside their emotions were swirling, but to get out of this, they'd have to find strength from somewhere. They'd have to try to swallow their sadness and be strong for each other … *try* being the operative word.

"Oh no? What do you call it then? She was down there with hundreds of those things, and I was all that was standing in between her and a horrible fucking end, and I dropped the branch 'cause just one of them came towards me. If that isn't cowardice, I don't know what is."

"Hey. Look. We need to move away from here," Gabby said, looking down into the pit as the rats desperately tried to scale the greased walls.

"Do you think they can get out?" Suzie asked.

"No," Gabby replied, "but we need to keep on moving. We're in the open here and they could show up any minute."

"Who? Who could show up?"

"I know a safer place. It was where we were heading when we stumbled across you. When we get there,

I'll tell you everything."

Suzie and Amber looked into the pit one last time. They hadn't been as close to Pip as Lauren, but they both felt sorrow welling in their eyes as they moved off.

Sal had to stay strong for her friend. She would mourn Pip when she had enough time to take a breath, but she had a sense that if this was the worst thing that happened to them today, they would be lucky. She placed a comforting arm around Lauren and coaxed her to follow Gabby.

Out of respect, Gabby did not run but walked swiftly in the hope that the others would do the same; to her relief they did.

Amber joined Sal and Lauren while Suzie jogged to catch up with the self-appointed leader. "So, you were pretty quick with that rat. Have you had to do that before?"

Gabby turned to look at her. She could see the pain on the young woman's face, she could see she was just trying to break the ice, make conversation, anything but think about what had just happened. "No. It was a first for me. The last twenty-four hours have been full of firsts."

"So what are you?"

"What am I?"

"Yeah, I mean, y'know, you're really fast; you've got this whole warrior chick thing going on. Are you like ex-forces or something?"

Gabby smiled. It was the first time she'd smiled since all this had begun. "I work as an order picker at a pharmaceutical warehouse."

"Okay, but you probably do survival weekends and stuff, yeah?"

"I spend my weekends drinking and watching movies, which I've usually forgotten by Monday morning. I'm an order picker. That's the full extent of what I do, unless you can call dodging phone calls from my mum a profession. Suzie, isn't it?"

"Yeah."

"I like your hair."

Suzie combed her fingers through her spiky pink razor cut. "Thanks. Still not a hundred per cent on the colour."

"Trust me, you'll be grateful for it."

The smile left Suzie's face. "What do you mean?"

"Well, if you all make it through the day, you'll be the only one left standing whose hair hasn't turned white."

10

Gabby led them through a narrow gap in a wide thicket. Lauren slipped her shoes back on, but the thorny branches whipped and lashed at her bare legs as they all struggled through. There was a dip on the other side, and the almost semi-circular bank was surrounded by even thicker bushes the rest of the way around, concealing it from any casual observer.

Gabby led them down to a cave entrance. "In here," she said, guiding the group in just far enough to be out of sight but not too far back to have no light.

"So, do you think you can tell us what the hell's going on?" Amber asked as they all perched down on rocks.

Sal placed a sisterly arm around Lauren who had not stopped crying since they had found her.

"Where do you want me to start?" Gabby asked.

"Well, the bit since we met you pretty much explains itself. Terror, rats, death, I mean that might just be me, 'cause I am a quick learner, but how about starting by how the fuck did we get here?" Suzie said.

"I don't know."

"So, what was all that shit about, I'll explain everything? I already know how to run, scream and cry. What else were you going to explain exactly?"

"It's good that you've got a sense of humour, you're

going to need it."

"How about you cut all this prophetic bullshit and give us some facts? What do you actually know?"

Gabby looked at Suzie and let out a long sigh.

"Okay. I was out on the town with a few mates. It was my twenty-fifth."

"Many happy returns," Suzie said. "How's twenty-five suiting you so far?"

"Thanks. Just great. I woke up the next morning out here, not remembering a single thing about the night before, other than meeting up with my friends and having a couple of drinks." Sal, Amber and Suzie all glared at one another. Even Lauren looked up for a moment as the words struck a chord with all of them. "Ah, I see that rings a bell."

"Yeah," Sal replied. "So, what happened then?"

"Well, they obviously like starting the proceedings with the rat pit, 'cause that was what brought all us together."

"Eh?"

"Oh yeah, and be careful by the way, those things are dotted all over the place. There are some bear pit traps too. You've got to be really mindful about where you're walking … or running."

"Good to know," Suzie replied.

"Yeah well, anyway, we could hear Olivia's cries for help long before we saw her. We kind of all converged at the same time. We'd woken up not knowing what the fuck was going on; then the screams started and they pretty much didn't stop."

"You said they," Sal said.

"What?"

"You said *they* like starting the proceedings. Who are you talking about?"

Gabby let out another sigh. "I don't know *who* they are exactly."

"Oh, that's handy," Suzie interrupted, "so—"

"If you'll let me finish," Gabby said, giving Suzie a

glare. "I don't know who they are exactly, but I've seen a few of them."

Sal placed a tighter arm around Lauren, who was now listening intently to Gabby's every word. "Excuse Suzie, please Gabby, she gets a little ahead of herself sometimes. So you've seen them. How? Where?"

"This is only just beginning for all of you, but I've been here a full day already. Trapping pits aren't the only thing out here you need to be careful about. I haven't seen any with guns yet, but that's not to say they won't have them."

"Who?" Sal asked more insistently this time.

"The hunting party."

11

"S'cuse me. Did you just say the hunting party?" Suzie asked.

"Yeah," Gabby replied.

"What, like with red coats, hats, horses and bloodhounds?"

"Err, no. I mean a group of guys, I've counted ten. They wear black, they wear ski masks, and they seem to hunt in pairs. They're well creepy, you can see their mouths and their eyes, and even that's too much sometimes. Two of them have crossbows, a couple have archery bows. Two have got what look like medieval maces, and four of them have these big samurai swords and a shit load of throwing stars."

A heavy silence hung in the cave while this information sunk in. It was Sal who broke it. "How many of you were there?"

Gabby dropped her head. It was the first time she had let her guard down enough to show her emotions. "Seven. There were seven of us. Like I said, Olivia was the first to go. Sasha was next, then they picked the rest of us off one by one. I found this place, and it seemed safe enough, but there was no way I was going to risk sleeping here by myself. I spent the night in a tree. When I climbed down the following morning … this morning, I went down to the stream to get a drink and came face-to-face with one of the fuckers. I don't know what made him angrier, the fact that I'd seen him without his balaclava on or the fact that I'd caught him taking a dump. Anyway, he went to grab his crossbow, and I knew I wouldn't be able to outrun one of his bolts, so it was instinct more than anything. I grabbed this piece of slate or whatever it is," she said, holding up the bloody, jagged stone in her hand, "and I stabbed the fucker. He fell back, his keks were still around his ankles. It would have been funny if it wasn't so fucking terrifying."

"Did you kill him?" Sal asked.

"I don't know. I didn't know if the rest of them were around, so I just turned and ran. When I saw you, I thought you were one of them, but as I got nearer, I realised you were just like me. I saw that bewildered, terrified look."

"Thank you," Sal said.

"What for?"

"For helping me."

"I'd save your thanks if I were you. The only thing I've done is delay the inevitable. We're trapped, we're outnumbered, and if we all make it through the day, it will be nothing short of a fucking miracle."

12

The remaining four friends looked at one another. Their eyes became cloudy with tears, but they fought them back. "Look, I'm not trying to scare you," Gabby said, "I'm not saying this for effect. I don't know where the hell this place is. I've not seen any fields or anything. All I've seen is forest … lots and lots of forest."

"You say there are more of those pits about?" Sal said.

"Yeah. We came across a couple of them. Jan fell in one, big wooden spikes at the bottom of it. It didn't kill her … don't know how, but it didn't. We killed her. We were trying to figure out a way to get her out, and the next thing we knew there were arrows sailing through the air towards us. We all scattered doing the whole running and screaming thing. After we regrouped, we carefully made our way back to the pit to find her there, arrow straight through her eye."

"I'm sorry," Sal said.

"What are you sorry for? They seem to enjoy this. They seem to enjoy breaking down your spirit, making you think that it's you that killed your friends rather than them." Gabby walked across to Lauren and crouched down in front of her. Even in the subdued light of the cave, she could see the tear streaks on the young woman's skin. She placed a gentle hand on Lauren's bare knee. "There's nothing you could have done; it was a rigged game."

Lauren looked at her for a moment. "I almost had her. If I hadn't—"

"No. That's what they let you think. They let you think that you're controlling your own fate; that you control the fate of your friends, but you don't. They control everything."

Lauren was about to say something else but instead just hung her head once more. "So, before we turned up, did you have any kind of plan?" Sal asked.

"Yeah. Not dying."

"No offence, but your plan lacks depth," Suzie interjected.

"Yeah, well, sorry I didn't have time to come up with a PowerPoint presentation for you, but they didn't let me bring my laptop. I don't know if you've noticed, but our resources are a bit thin on the ground."

"I think you've done amazing," Sal said. "You've

avoided them, you've hurt them, and you've saved us. Thank you. I know we're in a shit load of trouble, but thank you."

Gabby stood up. "Yeah, well, like I say, I don't really have any ideas beyond this—been too busy just trying to survive."

"How about …" It was the first time Amber had spoken in a while, and all heads turned towards her, searching her out in the subdued light of the cave."

"How about what?" Sal asked.

"How about we follow the stream? Gabby said there was a stream. How about we follow it? I mean, it must lead somewhere, and it's not like you can go around in circles if you're following a stream, is it?"

"I'm guessing you're the brains of the outfit," Gabby said.

"I know… I know, doesn't say a lot for the rest of them, does it?" she replied with half a smile.

"Actually, that's not a half bad idea," Gabby said, looking around at the others. "Anyone else got any thoughts?" Nobody spoke, but they all shook their heads. "Right then, the stream it is."

13

They remained in the cave for a few more minutes, catching their breath, mentally preparing themselves for the journey ahead. "You're not going to get far in bare feet or those things," Gabby said, pointing to the stiletto heels that sat on the rock next to Lauren.

"I don't really have a lot of choice, do I?"

Gabby bent down, gently lifting Lauren's feet and looking at the soles. "God, they're already cut to ribbons."

"I can't really feel much."

"That's only understandable, I suppose. Stay here a

minute," she said, standing once more and disappearing out of the cave.

Suzie walked across and sat down where Gabby had originally been sitting. "Are you okay, Lauren?" she asked tenderly.

"No," her friend whispered.

"Stupid question, I suppose. Look, we're going to get out of here. I've got a feeling in my bones," she said with a reassuring, albeit false smile.

Lauren stared at her for several seconds. "You can't really believe that. You heard what she said. You've heard who's after us. We don't stand a chance. They're going to get us one by one, just like they did with her friends, just like they did with Pip."

"No. We've got a plan now. We're going to find our way out of here."

"You hear that?" Lauren asked.

"What?"

"That sound … it's God laughing. It doesn't matter that we've got a plan. It doesn't matter if we have a dozen plans. We're screwed."

"I don't accept that. There's always a way."

"Tell that to Pip," Lauren replied bitterly.

"Look, Gabby told you there was no way you were going to save her. I mean they greased the sides of the pit for Christ's sake. That whole thing was like … an announcement or something, a big theatrical gesture to welcome us to the game and tell us that they were the ones in charge. Not you, not any one of us could have saved her."

"Theatrical gesture? Welcome us to the game? Have you heard yourself, Suzie?"

"Look, maybe that was a bad choice of words, but—"

"Duh, do you think?"

"My point is … what happened to Pip was beyond horrible, beyond a nightmare, and when we get out of here, we're going to mourn her properly, but it was like preordained. There was nothing we could do about it. We're all together now. We've got a plan, and we're going to head out of here. We'll keep our eyes peeled, we'll watch each other's backs, we'll be smart."

"Suzie's right," Sal said, leaning forward. She placed a gentle hand over Lauren's and squeezed it. "I'd kill or die for each of you. I love you guys, you're like my sisters … closer than my sisters. If we stick together, if we look out for one another, we can do this."

"You both seem very sure," Lauren said quietly.

"I am very sure; I've got a wedding in three weeks' time. You're my maid of honour," she said, looking at Lauren before turning to the others, "and you're my fucking bridesmaids. I've been planning this since I was about thirteen, so there is absolutely no fucking way I'm going to let these bastards ruin it." A small ripple of laughter travelled around the cave. Even Lauren smiled a little.

"Where's Gabby gone?" Amber asked.

"I don't know," Sal replied. "She told us to wait here and—"

"Does it bother anyone else that we've only got her word for all this?"

"What do you mean?" Sal asked.

"Well, she's told us the story of what happened to her friends, of how they died, of this weird hunting party, but…"

"But what, Amber?"

"But what if it's just that? What if it's just a story?"

14

A chilly atmosphere descended on the cave, and all four women looked at one another with unease.

"Okay, thanks, Amber, I think I've just shit myself," Suzie said. "What makes you think Gabby's behind

31

all this?"

"Well, I don't think it, I'm just saying, we don't have any proof. All we've got is her word for what's happened. What if all of this is made up? What if she's some kind of psycho and all this is a game to her? Or what if it's not all her, what if part of what she says is true but she's actually in league with them … she's one of the hunting party? What if she's out there now, rounding up her pals and they're all heading back here to finish us off?"

Suzie jumped to her feet. "Shit … she has been gone a long time."

Sal, Lauren and Amber all stood too. "What do you think we should do?" Sal asked.

"She hadn't thought about following the stream," Suzie said. "That was all Amber's idea. I say we fend for ourselves, find our own way out of here. If she's telling the truth, then she stands the same chance as the rest of us; if she's not then at least we've dodged a bullet."

"You don't think we should give her the benefit of the doubt?" Sal asked.

"Err, no. I'm interested in you, Lauren, Amber and me, that's it."

"But she tried to help me. If it wasn't for her—"

"If it wasn't for her, what, Sal?" Suzie interrupted. "What did she do exactly? She appeared out of nowhere and came charging towards you telling you to run. What did that save you from exactly? Run? Run from what?"

Sal's brow creased as she replayed the events in her mind. "The blood … the sharp stone and the blood on her vest … that ties in with her story."

"It tells us nothing at all. That could have been fucking Thumper the rabbit that she chopped up for all we know. Jesus, we can't take her at her word. We don't know her. We know each other, we know we can rely on each other. After what happened to Pip, I say that should be the full extent of our trust circle."

"Suzie's right," Amber began, "as much as I hate to

say it, I think we should take our chances by ourselves."

"Okay, that's two for leaving, what do you two vote?"

"Vote?" asked Sal. "You really think we can just decide like that with no more than two minutes of conversation? If she's innocent, if what she says is true, we can say she's got as much chance as us, but really we're sentencing her to death."

"Yeah," Lauren said, quietly, "but what if it's not true? We're sentencing each other to death."

"So what are you saying?"

"I'm sorry, Sal, I'm with Suzie and Amber on this one. It's just too much of a gamble."

"Okay, so say we decide to set off and follow the stream … where the hell's the stream? I haven't seen it. Have you seen it? Do you know what direction to go in?"

The other three looked at one another. "How hard can it be?" Suzie replied. "I say we get out before she comes back. At some stage, we'll find it, and if not, we'll figure something else out."

Sal let out a long sigh. "I feel really shitty about this."

"Shitty about what?" asked Gabby as she reappeared in the entrance to the cave.

15

The four friends all looked at one another nervously. "Listen," began Suzie, "we've—"

Gabby put her hand up, letting out a snarky laugh. "Don't worry, I won't make you cringe, I heard a lot of what you said, and you're right. If I was in your position, I'd be thinking exactly the same thing. You don't know me from Adam, and it does sound far-fetched; hell, if I hadn't lived through it, I wouldn't believe it myself. I doubt if there's anything I can say that will change your mind until shit actually starts happening, until arrows and bolts start flying in your direction."

"I'm sorry," Sal said.

"No hard feelings," Gabby replied, stepping further into the cave. She walked towards Lauren and tension immediately began to mount. Suzie took half a step forward, like a lioness defending her cubs. Gabby stopped and put her hands up disarmingly. In one of them there was a wad of thick, leathery looking leaves and a few long strands of tough-looking scrub grass. "Whoa, it's okay, I know when I'm not welcome. I got these for your friend. I thought you could use them to pad her feet and then maybe one of you nice ladies would let her have your socks. They're not exactly Filas, but it will give her a little padding." Gabby laid them down on the nearest rock and backed away. "Good luck, you guys." She turned around to go.

"Wait a minute," Sal said.

Gabby stopped. "Let me guess, you bought me a leaving present," there was a bitter smile on her face as she spoke.

"I'm sorry."

"I'm sure you are, but trust me, before today's over, you'll all be an awful lot sorrier." With that, she turned once more and headed out of the cave.

The heavy atmosphere lingered, and none of the women moved for nearly a minute. "What the hell was that supposed to mean? Before today's over, we'll be an awful lot sorrier. Shit, I told you, she was one of them," Suzie said.

"It didn't mean that. It meant we'll be sorry that we didn't trust her," Sal replied.

"That's not what it sounded like to me."

"Or me," Amber added.

Sal looked to Lauren. "What do you think?"

"What does it matter? We've made our choice, now we need to live with it and find our way out of here."

"You're right I suppose. You'd better sit yourself

down. Let's get those feet bandaged up," Sal said.

Lauren sat down on one of the rocks, and Sal and Amber got to work manufacturing the makeshift sandals. Suzie sat down on the opposite rock and slipped off her trainers, removing the bright pink socks that matched her hair perfectly. She brought them up to her nose and sniffed. "Sorry, these smell like Gorgonzola dipped in farts."

The other girls giggled. "You are so gross sometimes," Amber said.

"Just telling it like it is." She threw the balled socks across to Lauren, who plucked them out of the air with lightning reflexes.

"Thanks … I think."

"Y'know, one thing that Gabby chick was right about regardless of anything else. What happened to Pip wasn't your fault."

Lauren smiled weakly. She knew her friends were doing their best to make her feel better, but she also knew that whatever they said, she would carry those images, those screams and that guilt around with her for the rest of her life, no matter how long or how short a time that was.

Sal and Amber finished tying the makeshift sandals to Lauren's feet, and each of them unfurled one of the bright pink socks, carefully manoeuvring them under and over their friend's toes, soles and finally heels, doing everything they could not to snag or tangle the bindings.

"Try that," Sal said.

Lauren stood up and walked a few metres into the cave then back again. "It feels a lot better."

"You're a good liar."

Lauren smiled. "Well, it feels better than it did."

"That's something, I suppose. When we get to that stream, we'll clean you up. You've got some nasty scratches on your legs."

"Thanks, Sal. Thanks, Amber. Thanks, Suzie." Tears welled in Lauren's eyes again.

"Hey, come on. Whatever this is, we're going to get

through it," Sal replied, wrapping her arms around her friend.

"Definitely," Suzie added. "All for one and all that shit. We're going to get out of here. We're going to get the police, MI5, MI6, fucking James Bond on this and we're going to get justice for Pip. Whether it's one crazy bitch or a gang of howl-at-the-moon whack jobs, they've just messed with the wrong chicks."

16

The ebullient mood dissipated as soon as the four women stepped out into the open. They headed up the shallow embankment and trudged back through the thicket. Suddenly they felt much more vulnerable, much more on display. All four of them cautiously surveyed the surrounding landscape, looking for anything out of place— a colour, a movement, a shape.

"Which way then?" Amber asked.

"One way's just as good as another," Sal said, taking the lead.

There was no well-beaten path, merely one that had been insinuated by a thousand small creatures of the forest. They had been walking for a few minutes when Sal bent down and picked up a fallen branch. It came up to shoulder height and other than a slight bend in the middle was relatively straight. She held it out in front of her, gauging the feel and weight of it in her hand. "Thinking about Steve, are you?" Suzie said, and the girls laughed. Sal bent down again, grabbed a small twig, and held it out in front of her. "I am now."

They laughed once more; then a big crow flapped its giant wings, making them all spin around. It emerged from behind a bush and disappeared through the canopy. The four women turned back to one another, the smiles instantly becoming nothing more than memories. No matter how much they pretended this was a girl's day out, the reality was something very different. Sal dropped the twig on the ground.

"Jesus. I don't know about anything else, but I'm going to have a heart attack before this day's over," Suzie said, looking towards the sky.

"I know we don't really know what's going on, but Gabby said that there were more of those pits. Might not be a bad idea for all of us to have something to feel the ground out with … maybe use as a weapon if we need to," Sal said.

"I don't want to piss on your sparkler, Sal, but a mossy branch isn't going to be much of a defence if what she said is true," Suzie replied.

"Sal's right," Lauren said, picking up another chunk of tree just a little longer than the average cricket bat. She swung it using both hands, measuring what kind of weapon it would be if the occasion arose.

Amber didn't say anything, but seeing her two friends growing in confidence a little, she searched the forest floor until she found something too. The three of them looked towards Suzie, whose shoulders dropped. "Okay, okay." A moment later, they resumed their journey.

"Where do you think we are?" Lauren said.

"We're in the middle of a huge fuck-off forest," Suzie replied.

"Thanks for that. No, I mean … there aren't that many forests near us. We live in the middle of a city for Christ's sake. This place isn't some cute little nature trail, it's a proper forest, a big one."

The cocksureness disappeared from Suzie's face. "Err … well, I suppose it's a lost time issue, isn't it?"

"What do you mean?"

"I mean what's the last time any of us remember looking at a watch or a clock last night?"

The four women continued walking, desperately searching the memories of the previous evening. "I dunno, ten maybe," Sal said.

"Any advance on ten?" Suzie asked. Nobody replied. "Okay. Let's say it was about ten, ten thirty-ish then. I'm no expert, but I'm guessing it's maybe nine o'clock-ish now. Say for the sake of argument they planted us an hour or so before we woke up. That gives them a maximum of nine hours more or less."

"Jesus! We could be anywhere," Amber said.

"For the time being, I don't think where we are is the main issue," Sal said, coming to a stop.

"What do you mean?" Suzie asked.

Her friend didn't say anything, she just pointed. All their eyes followed the direction of Sal's finger; amid the green/brown landscape it took them a moment to focus on what had caught her attention, but then they saw it as clear as day. About thirty metres ahead of them, a single arrow was sticking out of the ground.

17

All four pairs of eyes darted in every direction, looking for the owner of the arrow. "Okay, there are two possibilities," Sal said, trying to stay as calm as she could.

"We're listening," Suzie replied, clutching the branch she had scavenged from the forest floor as if it was some kind of comfort blanket.

"Well, this could be coincidence. It might be a leftover from when Gabby and her pals were attacked ... *if* Gabby and her pals were attacked."

"And option B?"

"They're tracking us. They're watching us right now ... whoever they are."

Instinctively the girls formed a back-to-back circle. They scoured their surroundings harder than ever. "What should we do?" Amber asked.

"Anybody see anything?" Sal asked.

"No."

"No."

"Nada," Suzie replied. "But I did notice you didn't answer Amber's question."

"Since when am I the team leader?" Sal asked.

"Let's face it. You're the smartest one here."

"Okay, I still don't see how that qualifies me."

"Fuck me, Sal. Is it really the time for this discussion?"

"Suppose not. Well, to answer your question, I don't know."

"That's handy."

"There are a couple of ways to look at this."

"Which are?"

"If that arrow was put there deliberately, it could have been to make us think twice about going in that direction. They, Gabby, whoever, might be trying to coax us into a trap."

"So you're saying we should continue in the direction of the arrow?"

"No," Sal replied, "I'm just saying that could be one of the reasons."

The four of them continued their vigil, scanning every tree, every bush, every shadow. "I'm probably going to regret asking this," Suzie said, "but what could be another reason?"

"Remember that time we were walking in the park with your Benji and that bullmastiff sniffed around him and then put his paw on Benji's back nearly pinning him to the floor?"

"Err … yeah."

"When we got back home, we googled it to see what the fuck it meant."

"Shit. I was right, I do regret asking."

"Okay, you've lost me," Lauren said. "What did it mean?"

"It meant it was the bullmastiff's fucking park and he could do exactly what he wanted," Suzie replied.

"I'm with Suzie, I could really have done without hearing that particular hypothesis too."

"Okay, Sal. This is your call. What do we do?" Amber asked.

"Fuck it! Stay here." Sal marched off in the direction of the arrow.

Almost sensing the break in the circle, the others turned to watch her with disbelief painting their faces. "Sal? Sal?" Lauren called after her.

Sal reached the shaft sticking up from the ground and stood there for a few seconds, searching the vicinity to see if anyone revealed themselves. She reached down, wrapping her fingers around the carbon fibre missile, and tugged it free from the ground. She remained there a moment longer, waiting ... testing the water. The tiny hairs on the back of her neck bristled, but nothing happened. It was the easiest thing in the world to let paranoia run riot at a time like this. She exhaled a long deep breath and looked towards the others, who now regarded her with a sense of awe.

"Turns out it was just coinc—" Her eyes glared past her friends as a figure sprang into her field of vision. It was almost an action replay of earlier on that morning.

"Ruuun," Gabby shouted. "Run for fuck's sake!"

18

Sal froze for a split second as her friends began to charge towards her. Gabby was a good thirty metres behind for the time being, but she was running fast and getting faster. *Is this a trick?* Sal waited until her friends were nearly upon her then she turned and started sprinting as well.

They flew past the spot where she had uprooted the

arrow, which she still held firmly in her hand, and they kept going. The way ahead seemed clear, but maybe that was the whole point. *If it is a trap it's not going to fucking look like one, is it?* She cast a look back to Gabby who was still sprinting flat out. There was fear on her face, but if she was acting, or if she was some kind of psycho, that would be easy to manufacture. Sal looked behind Gabby and saw nothing. *This doesn't feel right.*

She turned back to her direction of travel, Amber had dropped her branch and was racing ahead. Suzie stayed back, conscious of the fact that Lauren was struggling due to her makeshift footwear. Whatever this danger was, no way was Sal going to leave her friend's side. She slowed a little more.

"Come on, Lauren. We need to go faster," Sal said, and Suzie placed a guiding hand on Lauren's back.

"I can't, my feet are agony," she replied.

Sal couldn't argue, even with her Docs on she could feel the odd jutting stone stabbing at her soles and heels. "Just try," she said, slowing a little more, realising that at any moment her friend could sprain her ankle or fall; then it would be down to her and Suzie to pick up the pieces as Amber tore further and further ahead.

Sal threw another glance behind to see that Gabby had gained further ground. She was still carrying the sharp bloody stone in her hand, although it looked like she had fashioned a handle for it now. *She's obviously watched too many* Rambo *movies.* An uneasy feeling gripped Sal, and she turned to look towards Amber. *Idiot, we're being herded. If all this is her, we're going exactly where she wants us to go.*

"You should leave me. I'm slowing you down," Lauren said in between pained breaths.

"Screw that," Suzie replied.

"Amber! Amber! Slow down!" Sal shouted, frantically scanning the track ahead for any signs of one of the pit traps. *Any second, Amber is going to disappear from view. She's going to become rat food and—*

Reality ceased to exist at that moment. All of them came to a juddering halt. A shining blade sliced through Amber's neck. It was a surgical incision. Her head somersaulted backwards through the air. Her open mouth expressed the nanosecond of shock she experienced before her body collapsed forward and crashed to the earth with a hollow thud. Her head continued spinning, spraying a small fountain of blood with each rotation and painting a gory trail across the forest floor. Eventually, it thumped against the ground, causing a small explosion of leaves and twigs in its wake. It continued to roll, toppling over the edge of the track and running down the incline. It was still gaining speed when the three friends lost sight of it.

Sal looked back towards Gabby. She had stopped running too; the same look of horror adorned her face as Sal's. She was not a part of this. Sal turned just as a black-clad figure emerged from behind a tree. Even from this distance, they could see the blood dripping from the otherwise glinting blade. The imposing figure wore a ski mask just as Gabby had warned.

"Shit. Everything she said is true," Suzie whispered.

As much as all of them wanted to run, they could not pull their eyes away from the man who was standing like a huge, menacing gargoyle in front of them.

Five seconds ran to ten, fifteen, twenty, and then the figure began moving towards them.

"This can't be happening," Lauren said quietly.

"It is happening. C'mon," Sal said, almost spinning her friend around. They started running in the opposite direction towards Gabby, who was still glued to the spot, hypnotised by the slow-moving, sword-wielding maniac.

Gabby tilted her head like a confused dog. *Why is he walking so casually? He'll never catch up.* A sudden and unfamiliar sensation cloaked her. She felt goose bumps bristle down her back then drew her gaze from the swordsman to the three girls. They had stopped running again. Their mouths gaped. *What was that look on their faces?*

Horror? Pity? A combination? It didn't make sense. She felt something wet press against her side, and she looked down. An arrow shaft was sticking out of her. Fresh blood was spreading in an ever-widening circle, and more still was running down her jeans.

"Fuck!"

19

Sal, Lauren and Suzie stared towards Gabby then followed the incline upwards. They could just make out a second black figure between the trees. As they watched, he nocked another arrow.

"Gabby, run! RUN!" Suzie shouted.

Gabby's face was getting paler by the second, she stumbled forward a little then veered off the path. Any second she would trip and drive the arrow in further.

"Shit!" Suzie spat. "Take Lauren. I'll get Gabby." She sprinted towards the wounded woman as the second arrow launched.

Sal looked back to see the swordsman had speeded up. "Fuck, come on." She placed her free hand around Lauren's waist, and they turned, immediately starting to run down the steep bank, quickly losing the power to come to a controlled stop even if they wanted to. They weaved in and out of the trees. She looked back. He was following for the time being, but he was not as agile as they were, he did not seem as willing to give in to the powers of gravity. "Come on, we can do this."

***

Gabby stumbled again, and the arrow missed but almost brushed her shoulder. Out of the corner of her eye, Suzie could see him nocking another. "Get behind a tree, Gabby!" she yelled. She watched as the wounded woman ducked out of the archer's line of sight. A victorious smile started on Suzie's face, but it vanished in less than a heartbeat as she saw him sweep the bow around and aim it straight towards her. "Oh, fuck!"

The missile was flying in Suzie's direction before she could even let out a breath. Instinctively she dived to her side, smashing against a tree. She let out a loud cry of pain, and the arrow whistled by, eventually burrowing into the earth. She broke cover, sprinting across to Gabby. Suzie looked up to see the archer retrieving a fourth arrow from his quiver.

"I … don't feel good," Gabby said, clutching her side.

Suzie looked at her wound. *Holy shit, she's losing a lot of blood.* "You'll be fine, it's just a scratch. Look, I'm a nurse, we'll get away from these mad bastards and get you patched up." Another arrow sailed dangerously close by. "Fuck me, that was near one. Come on." She grabbed Gabby's forearm, and the pair of them began to run down the hill, zigzagging between the trees, making it impossible for the archer to get a clear shot.

The incline got steeper, and every impulse in Suzie's body was telling her to put the brakes on before she was completely out of control, but the sound of a woman's scream pushed her to move even faster.

***

He came out of nowhere. This one was more than tall, and if he hadn't jumped out when he did, it wouldn't have taken Sal and Lauren long to spot him lurking. He was just three metres from them as he raised his sword high above his head. The balaclava did not hide the ill intent behind his piercing brown eyes. As his arms rose, so too did his black sweater, revealing a pale, fat, hairy belly.

Momentum was still carrying both women down the hill at breakneck speed. Sal didn't think, she just did it; she thrust the heavy branch she was carrying out in front of her, and before the swordsman could bring his weapon down, the point struck him. She hoped it would knock him off balance, give them enough time to escape, but so fast was the sequence of events that she misjudged the angle. The branch pierced the man's throat, and the force of the downward thrust kept it going, pushing it through the other side.

It was then and only then that both girls put on the brakes, digging their heels into the ground.

20

Suzie's heart was beating faster than ever. The scream had come from somewhere to her left, it sounded an awful lot like Lauren. *Please let them be okay, please let them be okay.* Gabby was starting to slow as the initial wave of panic and surge of adrenaline was giving way to the very real loss of blood.

"Come on," Suzie ordered pulling Gabby's arm even harder. The steepness of the hillside alone should have been enough to keep her going, but as she looked across, she could see Gabby had turned as white as a sheet. Suzie looked back up the bank. There was no sign of the archer for the time being, but that did not mean he wasn't after them.

"Leave me," Gabby said weakly, slowing down further.

Suzie reached out, taking hold of a low-hanging branch to act as a brake. It felt like her hand was being sandpapered, but it worked as she managed to force herself to a stop. Gabby fell back onto her bottom and raised her right hand. "What are you doing?" Suzie asked.

"Take this. It isn't much, but it's something." She handed Suzie the makeshift knife.

Suzie was about to protest when she saw Gabby's eyes expand to the size of Ping-Pong balls in fear. Suzie spun around to see a lithe but threatening figure advancing up the hill towards them. Like the others, he was dressed entirely in black. In his left hand he carried a sword, and as he passed through the intermittent rays of the sun that cast down through the canopy, it glimmered threateningly. His right hand reached to a small pouch on his belt and retrieved something that Suzie couldn't quite make out … well, for a few seconds anyway.

"Aaarrrggghhh!" It seemed more like sleight of hand than an actual throw. A barely noticeable flick and suddenly a metal star was sticking out of Suzie's shoulder. "You fucking cock-knocker," she growled angrily. The would-be assassin continued towards her, but now an amused grin punctuated the blackness of the ski mask. He reached for another throwing star. "Come on, Gabby, please we need to—" She looked back towards the wounded girl, but she wasn't just wounded any longer. Suzie had seen enough dead people in her profession to know when someone was beyond help. "Shit!"

***

The milky-skinned pseudo samurai collapsed to the ground at the same time the two women skidded onto their buttocks. They each clawed at the earth to halt their descent. They would have stopped for a moment to gather themselves, to take in the enormity of what had just happened, but Suzie's second scream of agony jolted them into action.

They jumped back to their feet, each glancing up the hill to see if the first swordsman was still after them. The way was clear for the time being. Sal was about to tug her spear back out of the man's neck when she realised there was a much better weapon at hand. She grabbed the sword, and the two of them immediately started running in the direction of their friend's cry.

***

Suzie was certain the maniac who was approaching her was playing a game. The second throwing star landed just two centimetres from the other. It was as if he was using her for target practice. The pain was unreal, but then her anger took over. The grin widened on her attacker's face. "Oh, you think this is funny, do you? You sick little shit stain. I worked on a psych ward; do you think I can't spot someone who channels his insecurity over having a dick the size of a cocktail sausage through violence against women?" His ear-to-ear grin vanished in an instant.

"Suzie!" It was Sal's voice calling from somewhere to the left.

The man's head shot to the side; then his eyes focussed on Suzie once more. "Not smiling anymore. Did I strike too close to home? Was that it? Used to get laughed at in the shower after P.E.?" Suzie could feel his hatred burning holes through her. It was her turn to smile. "I was just saying it to piss you off, who'd have thought I'd have struck an accurate diagnosis first time?"

He reached into the pouch once more, this time retrieving a throwing dagger. *Shit! That will do more than hurt.*

"Suzie!" Sal's voice was closer still now.

The shout diverted the swordsman's attention again, and Suzie dropped the branch, took one huge, fast stride and leapt. "Aaarrrggghhh!"

21

When their friend had not responded to the first shout, a feeling of despair cloaked Sal and Lauren. Had she become a victim of these sick killers as well? They continued in the direction they had last heard her but slowed their pace, dreading what they would find a little more with each step. But then, as Suzie's defiant battle cry boomed through the forest, their spirits instantly lifted, and they both started to run once more. The discomfort for Lauren was intense as the uneven juts and dips continued to stab at her feet, but this was life and death, this went beyond mere pain.

***

The sword-wielding maniac turned his head back around just as the human cannonball struck him. "Aaaggghhh!" it was his turn to scream. Suzie took him completely by surprise. He had done this so many times before; never had the women attacked, never had they goaded and mocked like this one had. This wasn't meant to happen. He stumbled backwards but still she came, her razor-sharp, pink-painted fingernails finding the skin of his neck beneath the polyester ski mask.

He felt the back of his foot strike a sturdy exposed root and air rushed beneath him as he toppled. All the time this wild-eyed, pink-haired Amazonian kept digging her claws in deeper. He hit the ground with a heavy smack, his head bouncing painfully off a solid mound of earth. His body shifted a little further down the steep hill, his assailant riding him as if he was a human sled. The mad punk girl pulled something from her belt then raised her right hand into the air. *What was that she was holding?*

***

Sal and Lauren caught sight of the frenzied movement through the trees long before they reached it. As they got closer, their hearts lifted further to see it was their friend who had the upper hand. Then panic seized them just as quickly. Further up the tree-studded bank, they saw a figure, perfectly still, waiting. He had one knee on the ground, an arrow nocked in his bow and even from where they stood they could see he was pointing it directly towards Suzie.

For the time being, he was letting the proceedings unfold. He had not seen Sal or Lauren, and both women crouched down. "Shit, what are we going to do?" Lauren whispered.

"Stay here," Sal replied, immediately disappearing into the trees to their right.

"Sal? Sal? Oh shit."

***

For different reasons, Suzie and the man between her legs both screamed at the same time. "Aaarrrggghhh!"

It quickly became apparent to him what that thing in her hand was as it came down towards him like Thor's hammer.

Suzie was consumed by rage. All through growing up, she had severe anger management issues. Her mother and father had got her professional help. She had learned how to process her feelings, how to filter them, but this was no time to filter feelings. Two of her friends were dead because of these men. An innocent stranger who had lost her life trying to help lay murdered just a few feet away. This was not a time for feelings; this was a time for animal instinct. Her pack had been attacked, and now she was fighting back.

The jagged stone dagger plunged into the swordsman's eye socket, causing blood to spray up into her face like a geyser. His body convulsed beneath her as if a sustained ten-thousand-volt electric charge was passing through him. Despite the gory horror, a wave of relief swept over Suzie. But it lasted mere seconds as a stark warning cry chilled the marrow in her bones.

22

"Suzie! Get down," Lauren screamed at the top of her voice.

On seeing the knife thrust into the other man, the archer further up the hill had risen to his feet. Lauren's warning shout came at the exact same second that he released the bowstring, setting the arrow sailing through the woodland towards its target. Without pause, the man withdrew another and nocked it, bringing the sight window up once more in readiness.

***

If ever there was a time to have blind faith, it was now. Suzie dived forward and to the right. Her face chafed against the earth and a jolt of pain speared her as her wounded left shoulder brushed against the ground. The man she had stabbed continued to shudder and convulse as she heard a wooden clack in front of her. She looked up to see an arrow had pierced the bark of a tree. If she had delayed her actions by more than a second, it would have pierced her vertebrae, in all likelihood killing her.

Suzie rolled, rolled and rolled again, not daring to see where the arrow had come from, only knowing that she was in mortal danger. She shuffled to her knees and speed crawled across the forest floor. She knew another shot would come at any second, and if she didn't find cover, this time she would not be so lucky.

***

He couldn't help but smile. He had done this so many times before, but it made it so much more entertaining when the quarry had spirit. He held back on releasing the bowstring, this girl was quick as well as a fighter. No, he needed to figure out where she was going. His experience would tell him when the epiphany took place; he would see a momentary turn of the head before one final lunge for safety. He didn't care about the man she had killed; he'd only met him once and, in honesty, did not think much of him. He was safe, his teammate was safe, and that was all that mattered—well, that and winning.

There! That was it. Just like a tell in poker, the split-second head jerk towards a clump of wild roses. Three, two, one.

It was the strangest thing he'd ever felt; frigid cold and searing heat at the same time, a weird, sharp, unequivocal feeling accompanied by a flash of white fogginess. He released the string and watched as the arrow flew, not where he intended; in fact, it was a completely wasted shot. *Had the bow snapped?* Then he saw it … he finally understood—the blade of the sword was still travelling through him. Blood was spurting from the wound in his belly like an overworked garden sprinkler. He dropped the bow. He didn't mean to; it was outside of his control. Weakness, weariness and now pain… Agonising, hellish pain ravaged his senses going from feeling nothing to feeling everything in the blink of an eye. It intensified tenfold as his attacker ripped the balaclava from his head, exposing his true self to the world. He had lived behind masks all his life, it was where he was comfortable, but this one luxury had been robbed from him too.

He could feel the flaming rawness where the point of the sword had entered his back. He could feel the frigid steel turning his insides to ice beckoning him towards the long, cold sleep that was just moments away. More than any of that though, he could feel the hatred as his killer brutally twisted the sword setting light to every nerve ending in his body. "Aaaggghhh!" He fell to his knees and tears began to cascade down his cheeks. *No, you can't cry. That's not how you can be remembered.* "Please! Please!" he sobbed. *No. Don't make this any worse, don't beg, you idiot.* He continued to wail like a little child as his system gradually ground to a stop. He looked down at the protruding blade and blood sprayed in his face. It was the longest few seconds he had ever experienced in his life.

Then, as quickly as it had appeared, the blade vanished, causing him to collapse back, for the first time revealing the out-of-breath, bloody-faced woman standing over him with a look of pure loathing on her face.

23

Sal just stood there for a while, looking down at the pathetic figure as life drained from him. She watched the tears run down his blood-splashed face and smiled. "Oh, you're such a big man, aren't you, crying for your mummy?

You piece of shit." She was about to walk off, content in the knowledge that any minute the final death rattle would pass his lips, but then she stopped.

The ski mask that was still in her hand … it wasn't just a balaclava. A tiny cloth pocket had been sewn into the temple and something glinted, catching Sal's eye.

"Sal? Sal, are you okay?" It was Suzie's voice. Sal looked down the hill towards her as she popped her head up from the cover of the rose bushes, but for the time being, she couldn't answer, she was lost for words.

Eventually, her vocal cords started working again. "What the fuck?"

***

Suzie continued to gaze in the direction of her friend, concerned as to why she hadn't replied. She was about to head towards her when a noise from behind made her spin around. "Jesus fuck!" she cried, throwing her hand up to her chest. "Are you trying to give me a fucking heart attack?"

"Sorry," Lauren replied, stepping out from behind a tree. "What's wrong with Sal? Why isn't she coming down?"

"I was just about to go find out before you made me piss my knickers."

"Sorry," Lauren said again before looking at Gabby. "Is she dead?"

"Yeah," Suzie replied sadly.

"She was telling the truth all along."

"I know. It's shitty, we should have believed her."

"And Amber. They got Amber. I can't believe all this is happening."

"Me neither it's like something out of a—"

"You're not going to fucking believe this," Sal said, appearing from nowhere and making both women jump.

"Fuck me, I wish people would stop doing that." Suzie placed her hand on her chest again. "Fucking believe what?"

Sal held up the balaclava, placed her thumb and forefinger into the small side pocket and removed a tiny camera. "Fucking believe this." She dropped the camera on the ground and stamped on it. "I don't know what the hell is going on here, but it's really creeping the shit out of me."

"They're filming us?" Lauren asked disbelievingly.

"It looks like it. Chances are more of them will be on the way. We need to get out of here quick."

"Just a minute," Suzie said, walking across to Gabby and kneeling down. "Sorry sweetheart." She gently closed the dead woman's eyes then pulled off her trainers. "Lauren, take those things off your feet."

"I'm not going to take her shoes, Suzie. It's … it's not dignified leaving her like that."

"I'm pretty certain she doesn't give a fuck, and all I know is that if we get into another cat-and-mouse chase with these bastards, no way are you going to be able to keep it up for long in those things. Now, do as I say and get those socks off your feet."

Lauren was about to protest but conceded her friend was right. If she got caught, it probably wouldn't mean just her own demise but theirs too. She took the trainers and started putting them on. "Did you see where that other guy went?" Sal asked. "The one who got Amber."

"No. He's probably around here somewhere," Suzie replied, picking up her victim's sword and unstrapping his belt, in turn releasing the small pouch containing the remainder of the throwing stars and daggers. She attached it to her own belt and glanced up the hill. "Do you think we should take the bow?"

"Have you ever fired one?" Sal asked.

"No."

"Me neither. I think I prefer this," she said, nodding towards her sword.

Lauren finished tying her laces and stood up. "She was about a size bigger than me, but I stuffed a few leaves in the toes. It's better than what I had anyway. Is there a weapon for me?" Suzie handed her one of the throwing daggers. "Err … how come you two get swords and I get a tiny blade like this?"

"No offence, Lauren, but in a million years you wouldn't be able to bring yourself to kill someone, even if all our lives depended on it," Suzie said, suddenly realising the two throwing stars were still lodged in her shoulder. She grimaced, tugging one out then the other. They weren't deep, and the adrenaline numbed much of the pain, but her friends watched for a second in awe of her toughness.

When Suzie was done, Lauren remembered they were actually in the middle of a conversation. "I … I would. You honestly think—"

"Suzie's right. You're like the sweetest person I've ever met. Now come on, let's get out of here before the rest of them show up."

24

The three women turned and began to jog down the hill; once again the momentum drove them more than their muscles. They moved in silence, staying almost shoulder to shoulder as they travelled. Their eyes scanned the treescape like lasers reading a digital image. They made sure they didn't miss an inch. After what had happened to Amber, they could not afford a lapse in concentration.

Eventually, the slope became more gradual, and the sound of their feet thumping against the earth started to be drowned out by the trickle and flow of running water. They stopped when they reached the bank of the wide stream and swept the entire area. Suzie and Sal cautiously climbed down to the water's edge, cupping their hands and scooping up mouthfuls of cold, fresh water.

Lauren knew that drinking stream water without boiling it was a great way to get the runs or worse, but she already felt like she was the outsider after the comments the other two had made, so she did the same, not wanting to give them any more fuel for their argument. After they drank, Suzie cleaned her shoulder wounds; Sal washed the blood from her face and arms while Lauren cleaned her legs.

They were covered in scratches from climbing through the thicket to the cave, but the cuts that really bothered her were the ones made by the rat. Just the thought of the creature's filthy claws penetrating her skin made her stomach turn.

Sensing her friend's discomfort, Sal placed a reassuring hand on her back. "When we get out of this, we'll make sure you get all the shots you need. You'll be fine."

"When was your last tetanus jab, Lauren?" Suzie asked.

"About two years ago."

"That's good. Don't worry, you'll be fine. You handled it better than I could. If one of those things ran up my bare legs, no word of a lie, I would drop down dead."

The three of them smiled, but it only lasted a few seconds. "I still can't believe Amber and Pip are gone," Lauren said quietly.

"I can't believe any of this," Sal replied. "I'd say it was like some sick joke, but it's much more than that."

"You realise that they're not going to stop until we're all dead," Suzie added.

"Cheery thought number twenty-two. Thanks for that, Suzie, that's really helpful considering the situation."

"Hey look, I'm sorry, but I'm just being honest. We know for a fact there are a load more of them, and—"

"Gabby was here a while, and she said she only saw ten in all that time, so I'm guessing that's all there is … was … meaning there are another seven of them somewhere. If we can just find—"

"Sal dearest, you of all people seem to be forgetting one important fact."

"And what fact is that?"

"The cameras those guys have on. They're streaming somewhere, to someone."

"We don't know that. These sick fuckers might just be recording it for their own entertainment. We don't know anything other than what we see, so how about us not painting this picture any blacker than it already is? Two of our friends died today. Gabby, a girl who tried to do nothing but help us, but thanks to your paranoia we—"

"My paranoia? Amber made total sense with what she said. We only had Gabby's word for everything that was going on, which up until a little while back was still the case. I was more inclined to trust my friend's instincts and back her rather than some stranger, so how about you come down off your high horse for a while and—"

"My high horse? It's always the same with you. You're always looking for the worst in people, always looking for problems that aren't there, instead of opening your mind up to things that might be going on outside your narrow field of vision."

"Ha! If that isn't the pot calling the fucking kettle. How about you look beyond your narrow field of vision and see what everyone else sees where your fucking Prince Charming goes?"

"What the fuck is that supposed to mean?" Sal asked, facing up to Suzie.

"You're the only one who doesn't see it. He screws anything that moves. Jesus, Sal, on the night of your engagement party he asked me if I fancied—" She broke off and immediately looked away. "It doesn't matter. We've got bigger problems to think about at the moment," she said quietly.

"Go on." Sal's voice was more hushed too now, almost nervous.

"Leave it, Sal. I'm sorry; I shouldn't have said any of that."

"Tell me."

Suzie paused and let out a long breath. "He asked

me if I fancied going upstairs with him. He said that you were pissed and you'd never notice anything... He's not a nice guy, Sal."

25

A tear ran down Sal's face, and Lauren took hold of her hand. "Why didn't you tell me before?"

"I put it down to him being pretty drunk too. Then, as time went on, you just became more and more besotted, and I didn't want to break your heart. I kept giving him the benefit of the doubt, thinking he might change, but he hasn't. I'm sorry. It's not an easy thing to tell a friend."

Sal turned to look at Lauren. "Did you know about this?"

"No."

"In hindsight, telling Lauren would have been the smart play. She doesn't have a filter, she would have just told you the whole thing verbatim," Suzie said, smiling, but nobody followed her lead.

"Well, I suppose I know now," Sal replied, wiping her eyes.

"Listen," Lauren said. "I'm on Suzie's side with this one. That is a really difficult conversation to have with a friend. But right now, we need to forget about all of that. We're all under a lot of stress. We're going to say things we don't mean. We need to put all our squabbles ... everything behind us. If we don't all work together to get out of here, then we're not going to make it. We're going to end up like Pip and Amber and Gabby."

"Lauren's right," Suzie said weakly. "I'm sorry, Sal. My temper gets the better of me sometimes."

Sal took a deep, shuddering breath. "This day just keeps getting better and better."

"Come on, let's get moving," Lauren said, leading

Sal up the bank. The silence was even more noticeable as they continued downstream.

Suddenly, Sal came to a halt. "The bartender at Maxi's."

The others stopped too. "What about him?" Lauren asked.

"You know the one I mean. He thinks he's fucking Tom Cruise in Cocktail … always has his shirt open one button too many."

"I know who you mean, but why bring him up?"

"The last time I got a round in, he had the tray on the back counter, out of view. I remember thinking it was weird, 'cause they always have the trays on the bar. When he brought it to me, he'd put those stupid little paper umbrellas in every drink, it looked fucking ridiculous. I paid him, and I remember watching him walk to the till. There were two rough-looking bastards sat at the end, didn't look like they belonged there. As he was getting my change, he nodded at them, and they nodded back. At the time, I just assumed he was just signalling that he would serve them next. It was him. He's the fucking reason we're here."

"What made you think of that?" Lauren asked.

"It just came back to me. I've been wracking my brains trying to think of any strangers we bumped into, and all the time it was staring me right in the face."

"But to what end?" Suzie asked.

"Huh?"

"Why would he?"

"Why would someone hunt a group of women in the middle of a forest? Why would someone build rat pits? Why would someone film the whole thing on miniature body cams? I don't know why any of this is happening, Suzie. But I'm telling you now. He's the fucker responsible."

"Well, if we ever get out of here, before the police get to him, you, me, Lauren and a pair of scissors will pay him a visit first."

"It's a date."

They carried on walking, surveying both banks of the stream as they went, all the time expecting to see a figure in black emerge from behind a tree or for the ground to suddenly give way beneath them, but nothing appeared, and nothing happened.

"Do you think we've lost them?" Lauren asked.

"I don't know," Suzie replied. "It seems like we've been walking an awful long time."

The stream twisted and turned until they followed it around a bend and all three of them came to a halt. They looked at one another and smiled. The forest ended giving way to several metres of tall wavy grass.

There was a bridge running across the fast-moving water. Granted, there was a fence too, and the fence disappeared in both directions out of sight, but this was a sign of civilisation at least. They continued towards the chain links, and all three of them stopped just short as they peered through the gaps towards the road. Never had a strip of tarmac looked so beautiful.

"So, I'm guessing unless we want wet feet, we're going to have to climb this thing," Suzie said, reaching towards the metal links.

"Yeah, but I think the barbed wire's going to be a bitch when we get to th—" Sal's thoughts were cut short as there was an insanely loud buzz followed by an arcing flame as Suzie was thrown back from the fence and into the yellow scrub.

26

Sal and Lauren shot terrified glances towards one another before running across to their friend. Despite the trauma, Suzie still held the sword in her hand. It was hard to tell if her hair was sticking up more than usual, but her entire body was shaking uncontrollably. White froth dribbled from the side of her mouth, and her pupils were dancing in a hundred different directions.

"Suzie. Suzie. Can you hear me?" Lauren asked as she nervously reached out to take her friend's hand. Suzie didn't reply, but relief swept over Lauren when she didn't get an electric shock too. She had no idea if there would be some kind of residual charge left in Suzie but was so happy when she found that there wasn't. She turned Suzie's hand over to see cauterised lacerations where she had placed her fingers on the fence.

"Ouch," Sal said, cringing. "That looks terrible."

"I don't know what to do," Lauren replied.

"Me neither. Suzie's the nurse."

"Suzie … Suzie, can you follow my finger?" Lauren put her index finger up in front of Suzie's face and slowly moved it from side to side. At first, there was no response, her pupils didn't seem to be able to focus on anything, but then gradually they began to move in a more predictable manner, eventually focussing on the finger as it moved from side to side like a bat in a game of pong. "Okay, that's a good sign, isn't it? I mean that must be a good sign."

"I really don't know why you're asking me. I don't have a clue," Sal replied.

"Well, I mean, if she can follow my finger, then surely that means her brain's not totally fried, doesn't it?"

"Lauren, I don't know. I don't know about any of this. Err … yeah, probably, but I mean there are people with Alzheimer's and stuff, and they can do that kind of thing, can't they?"

The pair looked at each other just like they were two scared kids back at school.

A sound came from the back of Suzie's throat, and her lips moved a little, but neither of them could make out what she was trying to say. Lauren moved her head in close, positioning her ear just a couple of centimetres from her friend's lips. "I didn't hear what you said, Suze. Can you say it again?"

Warm air brushed against Lauren's ear, and the side of her head as Suzie whispered more clearly. "I've not got fucking Alzheimer's you cheeky twats."

Panic ran through Sal as she saw Lauren start shaking. "What? What is it? What did she say?"

Lauren raised her head, and Sal could see that rather than tears causing the exaggerated body movement, it was laughter. "It doesn't matter," she replied, gently stroking Suzie's head. "She's going to be fine."

27

Suzie remained on the ground for several minutes. Lauren made multiple journeys to and from the stream, firstly to quench Suzie's sudden thirst then to clean the wounds the best she could. Lauren tore the short sleeves from her dress and fashioned a bandage to cover the nasty burns her friend had suffered.

Eventually, Suzie sat up, still a little dazed but quickly returning to her usual self. "So, I'm guessing that means we're going to be getting our feet wet."

"How do you mean?" Sal asked.

"Well, obviously the fuckers have electrified the fence, so that's off limits; we're going to have to head into the stream and under the bridge."

Sal looked down to the stone-built structure. The narrow tunnel was not particularly long, but it was long enough for them not to be able to see the other side. "Are you sure you're up to it? I mean I could head through and see if I could find some help or something. Jesus, Suzie, you've just had like a million volts sent through you. Do you really believe you should be thinking about moving?"

Suzie looked down to the bridge then back to the woodland. "Trust me, if I have to crawl out of here on my hands and knees, I'll do it." They rested for a few more minutes; then Lauren and Sal helped Suzie to her feet. "I think you'd better take this," she said, handing Lauren the sword.

"I thought you said I didn't have the killer instinct."

"I'll be happy to be proved wrong on that one." Lauren took the sword and handed Suzie the small throwing knife, which she subsequently placed in her belt.

"Right then," Sal said, "let's get this show on the road."

The three of them headed down the bank and paused at the edge of the stream. After a few seconds, they stepped into the icy water, for the first time getting a view of the other side of the bridge.

"Oh well, that's just precious, isn't it?" Suzie sniped.

"Oh God," Sal whispered.

Lauren didn't say anything, she waded into the middle of the stream as the chilling water rose to just above her knees. She ducked down to make her way through the low arch and carried on the few metres until she reached the other end. Blocking her exit was not a chain-link fence but a thick grill. Even in the subdued light, she could see that it would take a tank to break through to the other side.

She died a little inside. There was no way out. They would be stuck in this forest until they were killed by those men or rats, or electrocution, or God only knew what else. She barely noticed the cold water as she turned and made her way back out into the bright sun.

"I'm guessing they're not tears of joy," Suzie said as she noticed the glistening streaks on Lauren's cheeks as she waded towards them.

Lauren didn't say anything; she walked straight past the other two, climbed out of the stream, up the bank and sat down on a wide, flat rock. Sal followed her, plonking herself down on the same rock and sliding her arm around her friend's shoulders.

"It's okay. We'll find another way."

A bitter smile appeared on Lauren's face. "Course we will."

"I mean it."

"There's a time for optimism, and there's a time for just accepting that you've been dealt a crappy hand, Sal."

"Yeah well, that time's a long way off yet. Look, we took three of those guys out by ourselves, one of them with nothing but a tree branch. This isn't over, and no way am I even going to think about giving up."

Lauren let out a snort of laughter. "Keep talking like that and even I'll start believing we've got a chance."

"Sal's right," Suzie said, making her way up the bank to join them. "Look, there can't just be a fence and no way in or out. I say we follow it. At some stage, we're going to find a gate, a barrier, an opening … something."

"Yeah," replied Lauren, "and what if they find us before then?"

"If they find us, they find us, but in my life I've never done anything quietly, and I'll be damned if I go without giving them hell."

28

With each minute that passed, Suzie felt a little stronger. She looked down at her wounded shoulder then to her hand. She wasn't quite sure which hurt the most, but now they were out of the trees and walking in the warm afternoon sun, her nerves were on a more even keel. There was a six-metre border between the forest and the fence. The majority of it consisted of scrub grass, with the last metre before the chain-link barrier being made up of pebbles. *Were they near the coast?* The road on the other side of the chain links still tantalised them. Freedom was so near and yet so far, but seeing an out-of-reach road was infinitely preferable to seeing the black-clad maniacs who had killed their friends.

Sal and Lauren walked on either side of her, clutching the swords like battle-hardened warriors, waiting for the next attack. "We haven't seen sight or sound of them in ages. Do you think this might be over? Do you think 'cause we killed three of them, they've just cut their losses and left us in here to slowly starve to death?" Lauren asked.

"Jesus, Lauren, you are such a child sometimes," Suzie said.

"Get lost, I was just—"

"A - It would take us forever to starve here. There are like berries and nuts and all sorts that could give us some kind of sustenance. There's even a fresh water supply, so unless they're planning on leaving us here until next winter, we'll be fine. B - Do they really strike you as the type of people who would just give up? I mean, Jesus, they've got a fucking electrified fence. They placed all these fucking traps; they've got bows and swords and fucking throwing stars. They obviously live for this shit, so, no, I don't think they've cut their losses. And C - Whoever they are, for whatever reason they're doing this, do you think they're going to leave witnesses?"

"Suzie's right. Christ knows how long they've been doing this, but they seem to be very organised, well-funded and, worse than any of that, I'm pretty certain they enjoy it."

Lauren thought for a moment. "So, if all those things are true, how come we haven't seen anything of them for so long?"

Suzie opened her mouth to answer but then closed it again just as quickly. The fact was she didn't have an explanation. It didn't make sense.

"I'm sure we'll find out soon enough, but let's just make the most of this while we've got it, shall we?" Sal said, gesturing around to the nothingness ahead and behind them.

They carried on in silence, keeping watchful eyes on the trees, making sure that no dark figures were loitering in the shadows.

It was Suzie who broke the tranquil mood. "Do you hear that?"

The other two stopped, angling their heads to listen to the sounds of the forest. "Hear what?" Sal asked.

"It sounds like some kind of buzzing noise."

"I don't hear anything," Sal said.

"Me neither," added Lauren. "Hey, I'm not trying to be funny, but could this have anything to do with the electric shock?"

Suzie looked confused for a moment, "No. Tell me you can hear it, it's getting louder."

"I really can't hear a thing," Lauren said.

"Me neith— oh shit. I can hear something. What is that?"

Lauren listened hard, and finally she could hear it too. "It sounds like … a hedge trimmer."

"Oh yeah, that's just what I was thinking. The blood-lusting maniacs who murdered our friends are probably just having a little downtime in the communal garden before they start round two," Suzie replied.

"Get lost. It does, it sounds like—"

"Shut up, the pair of you," Sal ordered as the sound gradually got louder. "It sounds like…"

"Hedge trimmers."

"More like a quad bike," Suzie said.

"No. It sounds like a model plane," Sal replied.

"What?" Lauren and Suzie asked at the same time.

"Y'know those model planes that the nerdy kids used to fly in that after-school club. The ones with the remote controls."

"Hey, wait a minute, Sal's right," Lauren said. "That's exactly what it sounds like."

"Oh shit. No, it doesn't. It sounds like a fucking drone," Suzie replied, turning her head upwards and to the left.

"How can you tell?" Sal asked.

"Because I'm looking at it right now."

29

All three of them just stared up in disbelief for a moment as it hovered. It was not so far off the ground that they could not see the camera looking down at them, but nevertheless they were glued there, spellbound.

"I suppose this means they've found us," Lauren said quietly.

"Do you think?" Suzie replied.

Lauren dragged her eyes away from the drone and set them on Suzie in a fearsome glare. "Just so you know; I'm getting really fed up of your constant sniping."

"Fine," Suzie replied, levelling up to her. "Then stop stating the bleeding obvious as if you're revealing the meaning of life. Of course they've found us. It's not fucking Amazon delivering my new iPhone case, is it?"

"You two, shut the fuck up. I'm getting sick of both of you. This isn't the time or the place. I think we've got bigger fish to fry, don't you?"

Both women's nostrils flared as they let out frustrated huffs; then their eyes rose to the hovering menace, which was still observing them. "So, what do we do?" Suzie asked.

"Well, my guess is it's going to stay on us. We might be able to lose it if we head into the trees, but then we're back to square one, just running, hiding and waiting for them to find us."

"This is surreal," Suzie said. "We're standing here, looking up at something that's looking down at us. All the time, those wankers will be closing in. They want us to head into the forest, 'cause that's where all the traps are, where they're strongest, and at the same time, that's the only possible way that we can lose the drone. They're trying to herd us again."

"Lauren, how far up would you say that thing is?" Sal asked.

"Not far … about five or six metres."

"I've seen you playing softball. When you get that ball in the outfield, you can chuck it for fucking miles."

"Well, yeah, but unless you've got something hiding in your bra, I think we're all out of softballs."

"There are a fair few pebbles over by the fence though, aren't there?"

"I suppose."

"You'd need to be quick, Lauren. You'd need to do it before they have a chance to figure out what's going on."

"What are you suggesting?"

"Suzie, fancy causing a diversion for Lauren?"

"What did you have in mind?" Suzie asked.

"Well, just imagine it's any Friday night in Manchester city centre and you've had too much to drink. Jesus, it's not fucking difficult, Suze, that's like every fucking Friday night for you."

"Screw you, Mother Teresa." Suzie looked at Sal and smiled then looked towards Lauren. "Don't fuck this up; we'll only get the one chance. Okay, give me a second to get into character. Three, two, one…"

30

Suzie reached around her back, unclipping her bra beneath her T-shirt; then she spun around like a wild animal. Her eyes fixed on the camera attached to the drone before ripping her T-shirt off and starting to shout at the top of her voice.

"You want something to look at, you bunch of fucking psycho pricks? Then fucking look at these!" she screamed, taking hold of her ample milky-white breasts and pointing them up to the camera. "You want to follow us around all day? You want to track us back through the forest? Well, good luck with that, y'cunts, 'cause I've fucking had enough. I've had enough of all your fucking bullshit. You hear me? I've fucking had enough. We all have. We're not falling for any more of your tricks; we're not going to walk into any more of your fucking traps. You want us, you come here and fucking get us." She finally took a breath and let go of her boobs but then started pointing her finger towards the drone. "Come on, I fucking dare you. Leave all your weapons back there and just come and face us, a proper fight. None of you would last five fucking minutes; I'd rip your fucking balls off and sell them to Campbells. They'd be served up with fucking spaghetti and tomato sauce before you knew what was happening, you bunch of fucking impotent mummy's boys. Come on. Come and have a go if you think—"

The pebble appeared out of nowhere. It crunched into the right front leg of the drone, smashing it loose from the body, causing it to dangle by one long wire. By some miracle, that particular propeller kept rotating, making the machine unnavigable. It began to spin and dip as the remote pilot tried hopelessly to control it. It was only a few seconds before it got tangled in the branches of a tree then finally clattered to earth.

"Yes! Nice work, Lauren," Sal said.

Suzie bent down and picked her T-shirt and bra up, carefully putting them back on, desperately trying to avoid the area where the throwing stars had caused lacerations. "Jesus, Lauren. Took you long enough. I was running out of material."

"Come on, Suzie. We all know that's a lie, you were having the time of your life. You could have carried on for another half hour at least," Sal said.

"I suppose," she replied, grinning. "Well done, Lauren. Nice throw."

"Right. Let's not waste the advantage," Sal said.

"Time to get the hell out of here."

Lauren picked up her sword, and the three women started running as fast as they could. For the moment, they were sticking to their plan. They stayed in line with the fence and the road. If the men in black appeared, they would probably have to come up with a fresh idea.

"How big is this place?" Lauren asked after they had been running for over five minutes.

"I was just wondering that myself," Suzie replied. "I think I'll need to slow down a bit. I'm feeling a bit dithery."

"Only to be expected after what you went through," Sal said.

They didn't stop entirely, but they slowed long enough for Suzie to get her second wind. "When we get a chance, I could really do with something to eat."

"Yeah, I think we all could," Sal replied. "Look, how about we carry on for another ten minutes or so then head into the woodland and see if we can find something?" Suzie nodded gratefully.

They hadn't been travelling for half that time when Suzie came to a stop once more. "What is it?" Lauren asked.

"I hate to sound like a broken record, but do you hear something?"

31

Sal and Lauren instantly came to a stop, desperately hoping that their friend was wrong this time. "Oh shit," Sal said. "I'd give anything to hear the sound of a drone rather than that."

The noise from behind them was of men shouting. They looked towards the path they had beaten through the long grass. "What a set of complete fucking donkeys. We should have run just inside the tree line or something."

"Hey look," Sal said, "it's not like we run for our lives every day, let's put it down to beginner's mistakes, and the thing is, if these guys do this all the time, once they got a clue as to where we were, it wouldn't have been that difficult to track us."

"I suppose you're right," Suzie replied. "So, what do we do?"

Sal looked back. The voices seemed to be getting nearer by the second. The men were probably rested, fed and watered; it would not take them too long to catch up. She looked into the forest. It was the last place she wanted to go. In there, there was no hope of finding a way out. In there, there were booby traps and horrific memories it would take her a lifetime to forget … of course, the way things were going, that was probably going to remain unprovable. The one thing the forest could provide was temporary cover. It might buy them just a little more time. She let out a long breath and shot one final look back to the way they had come.

"Well?" Lauren asked.

"I'm not happy about it, but it's our only option. We head into the forest."

Neither Lauren nor Suzie argued, they just followed, silently. All three women looked up towards the blue sky before heading in, all three realising it might be the last time they ever saw it.

Sal led the way, not knowing for a second where she was going. They kept a close eye on their surroundings. They didn't keep to a straight line. Sometimes they took the easiest path; sometimes they forced their way through spiny thickets. Within fifteen minutes, Lauren's bare legs looked like they'd been subjected to death by a thousand cheese graters. They carried on for another few hundred metres and found a small brook.

They stopped to take a drink, their heads twisting and turning like wild animals checking the area for predators. When they had finished, Suzie insisted that

Lauren sat down on a log while she cleaned her wounds. Considering she was a nurse, Suzie was not one of the most caring people in the world, so this was not just uncharacteristic; it was a massive gesture of goodwill on her part, maybe even an apology, although Suzie would never actually apologise verbally.

She washed her friend's legs and dabbed them with dock leaves. When she was done, she examined them more closely. They were still bleeding in places, but she could make a decent assessment of the damage. "Don't worry, hot stuff, you're going to be okay."

"Am I going to have scars?" Lauren asked.

"We need to make sure you get shots as soon as we get out of here." The words came out before she even thought about them. The likelihood of them escaping was diminishing by the minute, however, what was the alternative? "But the scratches are all superficial. They'll heal up in no time."

"Thanks, Suzie."

"Welcome." She stood up and was about to help Lauren to her feet when she stopped. "Err ... where the fuck's Sal?"

32

On hearing Suzie's words, Lauren didn't need any help, she sprang to her feet. "Oh shit. Sal? Sal?"

"Relax, I'm here," she replied, crouching down behind a thick bush.

"You dropping a chocolate penguin over there?" Suzie asked.

"You remember at my engagement party when your mum came up to me and asked why you couldn't find a nice boy to settle down with just like I had and I said I didn't know? I think I've just figured it out."

"There isn't a man on this planet that would make me want to settle down. I'm having way too much fun … well, I was anyway."

"For your information, I'm picking raspberries."

"I really hope you're actually picking raspberries and that's not a euphemism for something else that's totally gross," Lauren said.

Sal stood up. She had stretched her T-shirt out in front of her and allowed the excess material to sag in the middle creating a kind of sling for the fruit she had gathered. She carefully walked across, making sure she didn't drop any of the juicy bounty.

"Are you sure they're alright to eat?" Lauren asked.

"They're raspberries," Sal replied.

"Yeah, but y'know, they're just sitting out here in the woods. It's not like they've been tested or anything."

"Tested. Lauren, they're fucking raspberries. What the fuck are you going to test them for?"

"I don't know; it's just when you go to Tesco's or something, you know they're going to be okay, they're grown by farmers in fields and stuff. What if these are different?"

"Okay, Lauren, I love you, you're like a sister to me, but they're fucking raspberries. The only difference between these and the ones you get in Tesco is these aren't fucking three quid a punnet. Now grab a handful and eat them for fuck's sake."

They divided the berries up into three equal portions and greedily devoured them, all the time watching the woods around them for any signs of danger.

"That filled a hole … as the actress said to the bishop," Suzie said, doing her best to put a smile on her friends' faces. The smiles were not forthcoming. "Where next, captain?"

"I wish you'd stop saying that crap. We're all in this together. I don't have a plan. Sooner or later, those guys are going to come across us and then we're going to have to run or fight like we did last time. Considering six of us started out and in a matter of a few hours we're down to three, I don't really rate our chances too highly."

"Good pep talk," Suzie replied.

"Yeah, well, I'm just telling you how it is. We got away by the skin of our teeth."

"Whoever said honesty is the best policy was a dick."

"Come on, we should get going again," Sal said.

"Where?" Lauren asked.

"Weren't you listening to a word I said?"

"We've got to have some kind of plan, Sal. We can't just walk around in circles."

Sal didn't say anything for a few seconds, but her face turned bright red. "Okay, you want a plan, here's the plan." She violently plunged the sword into the earth, and the other two girls jumped back in surprise. "My plan is someone else can make the decisions, 'cause I've had a fucking belly full." A single tear rolled down her left cheek; then she turned and marched off through the trees.

33

Suzie and Lauren turned to look at one another in stunned silence. With everything else that was going on, the one they had always relied on to be sane, the sensible one, the brave one, was now going into meltdown.

Suzie tugged the sword from the earth, and she and Lauren ran after her. "Sal … Sal," called Lauren as the pair of them hurdled overgrown roots and weaved around trees.

"Fuck off. I can't take this. I can't take this anymore," she said, her voice shaking.

"Sal, slow down, please." They finally caught up with her and Lauren grabbed her friend's shoulder. As Sal turned, glistening streaks lined her face.

"Sal, don't cry. You know when you start crying, it always makes me cry."

"You keep asking me what next, what do I think we should do. How do you expect me to know?" She looked at Lauren and then towards Suzie. "I've got no fucking idea. What is it you expect from me? Why do you think I should know what to do out here?" she said, gesturing around her. "I mean, Jesus, I don't think I'd seen trees other than in a park until I was about sixteen years old. I grew up in a fucking concrete jungle, not a real one. What magic answers do you think I'm going to have?"

Lauren looked down at the ground. "I'm sorry. We shouldn't put you under that kind of pressure."

Sal looked across to Suzie, and for a split second she saw sympathy in her friend's eyes, but then it was gone. "Y'know what? Fuck you, Sal. You wanna go off on one and wallow in self-pity when we need you the most, then go ahead. And what you just said, that's the reason we look to you."

"What are you on about?" Sal asked irritably.

"Fuck me," Suzie said, "you really want to do this now?" Sal just looked straight at her. "Right, fine! Remember that weekend when we were fifteen and my parents went away? I held that party. There must have been thirty people there. You were so excited, you'd been looking forward to it all week 'cause you thought it was finally your chance to get off with Ricky Allen. Then some total twat spilt my dad's port over the new beige carpet he'd just had fitted in the living room. Fuck! I don't think I've ever been so upset in my life."

"I remember that," Lauren said. "I thought I was going to have to go home and get you some of my mum's valium."

"Yeah, well, I could have done with it. Anyway," she said, turning back to Sal, "you told me to move the party to the kitchen and not to worry … like that was fucking going to happen. You spent the entire night getting that stain out. That prick Ricky Allen disappeared halfway through with Debbie Holstead, but you didn't care. You just made sure that there was no sign of a stain. When the party was over, I'd got so fucking drunk that I could barely stand. You put me to bed, and when I woke up the next morning, everything had been tidied away, it looked like I'd had a fucking contract cleaning company in."

"Yeah, so? I got a stain out of a carpet, how does that qualify me to deal with this?"

Suzie looked at Lauren and then back to Sal. "Because that's what you always do. You take charge of a situation, and you do everything you can to help and protect your friends. You did it that night; you've done it a thousand times since. You always know what to do, and you always look after us. You practically raised yourself, Sal. God, if anyone has earned the right not to give a fuck about others, it's you, but that is the last person you are. That's why we always look to you, 'cause you're the one who's always been there for us. You're the one who's always looked out for us. And y'know what, you're right; it's time we started giving what we get, but right now, we need you more than ever."

The fight and frustration left Sal's face. She grabbed the sword back from Suzie. "Y'know, I really hate you sometimes."

34

They didn't talk for a while, they just moved. Sal was lost deep in her thoughts; as much as she didn't want to deal with this, it was hers to deal with. Born and bred in a block of council flats on the outskirts of Manchester city centre, with a jailbird father and a slapper of a mum, there were a million different terrible things that could have happened to her, but never could she have anticipated this.

"Shit!" Suzie hissed.

Sal stopped and turned to look at her. "What is it?"

"I can hear them again."

"Have you got cyborg ears or something?" Sal raised her head to listen. It took a few seconds, but she could hear someone calling instructions. "Shit," she said with a deflated breath. "Come on." They started running again. *This is mental. We're running to get away from them, but we don't know where we're running to. There's no way out of this fucking nightmare.*

Spindly branches whipped against them as they dodged in and out of the trees, but that was the last of their concerns. The men's voices gradually began to fade once more. Another few minutes and they could stop again, but the realisation that this game of cat and mouse could not go on indefinitely hung over them all like a gathering storm cloud.

A deafening crack erupted into the air and for a fraction of a second Sal thought someone was shooting at them. When she heard Suzie's sustained shriek of pain, she was convinced her friend had been shot, but as she turned around and saw Lauren skidding to a halt and no sign at all of Suzie, confusion swallowed her for a moment. *What the hell?*

"Sal! Lauren!" came the tearful shout, and that's when both friends noticed the narrow black hole that had appeared in the forest floor. "Be careful," she added in between sobs of pain.

The two girls walked across and tapped at the earth with their swords. Solid … solid … solid … hollow. Sal's blade broke through a thinly camouflaged trap door constructed of branches, leaves and dirt. Even when not travelling at speed, it was tough to see; it blended into the forest floor perfectly. She reached down and flipped open the concealed, crudely assembled construction, causing a small avalanche of debris to fall.

"Oh shit!" Sal and Lauren said at the same time.

Wooden spikes stuck out from the pit's floor by

about thirty centimetres. Suzie was standing at a diagonal, her right arm stretched out against one of the walls, her left leg planted dangerously close to one of the spikes, her right leg raised off the ground, the ankle jutting at an impossible angle. She looked up, but tears of pain flooded her eyes, all she could see were blurry outlines. "Help me … please."

35

Sal and Lauren continued staring down for a minute, trying to assess exactly what the damage was. "Did you land on one of the spikes?" Lauren asked.

"No," Suzie sobbed. "I don't know how, but no. My ankle's fucked though."

"Fucked?"

"Fucked—broken."

There was another pause. This was it. All for one, one for all, that would mean death now. Nothing was more certain. "I'll … I'll go find a branch," Lauren said.

The pit was about eight feet deep, the walls to this one had neither been greased nor tiled, it was very basic—you fall into it, you get spiked, you die, at least that should have been how it worked. "You were lucky," Sal finally said.

"Oh yeah," Suzie said, sniffing back her tears. "Must be the Irish blood in me from my gran's side. I feel proper fucking blessed. Remind me when we get out of here, I'll do the fucking lottery, it's obvious I'm leading a charmed fucking life today."

"I mean that was designed to kill you. To fall in there and not get speared … the odds must be a million to one."

"Your words aren't helping."

"I know. Sorry. Look, we'll have you out of there in a couple of minutes and then—"

"Then what? You carry me? This is the end of the

road … for me anyway."

She was only saying what they had all thought at that moment after it had happened, but it still made Sal angry. "Stop it. We'll figure this out."

Lauren came back with two long branches, placed her sword down on the ground and gave one of the branches to Sal. She put her own weapon down too, and they both lowered the sturdy boughs into the pit.

Suzie carefully pivoted on her good foot and placed her left hand against the wall to join her right. Her friends manoeuvred the branches until they were touching her fingers, and Suzie pushed herself off the wall and grabbed hold of them. "Okay, take it slow. I'm going to have to shuffle closer before you start lifting."

"Don't worry, Suze. Take your time," Sal said as her friend awkwardly skidded and hopped up to the wall avoiding the remaining spikes.

"Okay," she said and tightened her grip around the branches.

"Three, two, one, pull," Sal said through gritted teeth. She and Lauren let out loud grunts as they took Suzie's weight.

"Wah!" screamed Suzie as she shifted up the wall about eighteen inches in one fast, jerky movement.

"You okay?" Lauren asked.

"Yeah. Just took me by surprise, that's all. Please don't drop me."

"Hold tight."

Another sudden movement dragged Suzie even higher, and now her head rose above the edge of the hole. A third forceful tug and her chest and ribcage were out. So agonising was the pain in her ankle that she had all but forgotten the sore throwing star wounds in her shoulder and even the burns on her hands. Lauren and Sal pulled one last time, and now it was just Suzie's legs from the knees down that dangled over the mouth of the pit.

Her two rescuers dropped the branches, bent down

and heaved Suzie completely clear. They looked at her misshapen ankle, and a sudden queasiness came over them both as they threw each other sad glances.

Suzie rolled over onto her back and stared at her feet. Tears were still running down her cheeks, and on seeing the full extent of the damage to her ankle, the narrow streams suddenly became rivers.

36

Sal and Lauren sat down beside Suzie. Each of them took one of her hands in their own and caressed it gently as she continued to cry. A couple of times they opened their mouths to say something comforting, but when no words came, they closed them again.

Eventually, the initial trauma wore off, and the tears of shock and horror turned to tears of pain before eventually becoming just salty streaks.

The three of them remained there for several minutes. Even when the shouts of one then two men were heard not too far away, they stayed put. What could they do? They couldn't exactly run to safety, not now. Sad resignation shrouded them.

"I'm sorry," Suzie said weakly.

"What are you sorry for?" Lauren asked.

"If I'd have been paying proper attention, this wouldn't have happened."

"Any one of us could have fallen down that hole. At least you were quick thinking enough to remain upright; you could have been a goner down there."

"Oh yeah, this worked out so much better." She let out a shuddering breath. "I want you two to go."

"Fuck off," Sal spat. "We're not leaving you. Look, maybe we can find somewhere to hide," she said, desperately searching around. All she saw were trees, not

79

even any thickets or sprawling bushes.

"I've already looked, Sal, there's nowhere."

Sal stood up, grabbing one of the branches. "I've got it," she said, looking across to an old willow. "Me and Lauren will climb into the tree then pull you up. That'll work."

"Suppose it does," Suzie asked. "What then?"

"Well, it buys us a bit of time to come up with something."

Suzie gazed at her ankle once more then up to her friends. She really loved them. Sure, they had their fallouts, they had their problems, but they were closer than blood.

"Okay, help me up," she said sadly.

37

Lauren and Sal helped Suzie to her feet and gave her the two thick branches to use as crutches. It wasn't much of a plan, but it was a plan at least. When their friend was vertical, they picked up their swords and walked to the tree to figure out the best way to proceed.

"I was never great at climbing trees," Lauren said, tapping one of the lower boughs with the sword to get an idea of its sturdiness.

"Listen, I'll climb up first; then, when I'm in position, I'll pull you up, and then we can both get Suzie up."

Lauren carried on looking at the tree for a moment, but when another shout from one of their pursuers carried on the breeze, she snapped out of her thoughts. "Okay, let's do this," she said, turning around.

She and Sal froze. Suzie was standing at the far end of the pit. The makeshift crutches were firmly beneath her armpits, propping her up. She had removed her belt and was holding the small pouch of throwing stars and knives in her hand.

"Suze, what are you doing?" Sal asked, her heart pounding in her chest as she saw a different kind of sadness in her friend's eyes.

Suzie flung the small belt bag to the ground then shuffled forward a little more.

"I love you guys. I won't let you die for me. Tell my mum and dad what I did here. I might finally be able to make them proud." With that, Suzie raised her arms a little and the branches fell away. She tipped forward on her one good leg and like a chopped tree fell into the pit.

"Nooo, nooo, NOOO!" Sal screamed. It echoed around the forest, causing birds near and far to take flight. She and Lauren ran to the hole in the ground, but before they reached the edge, there was a shallow, pathetic cry and a loud wooden thump.

Both of them turned away with fresh tears pouring as the image of their friend impaled on spikes burned enough terror into their memories to last a hundred lifetimes.

Lauren picked up the pouch Suzie had dropped and grabbed a tight hold of Sal's upper arm. "Come on," she said, still sobbing.

Sal struggled free. "No, there's no point. It's all over."

Another shout, the hunting party was much closer now.

"She died to save us. If we let them catch us now, it will have been for nothing. At least let what she did buy us a little time if nothing else, Sal. We owe her that."

Sal glared into the pit. If the spikes had been two feet long instead of one, in that split second she might have dived in too. "I'm so sorry, Suzie."

Lauren took hold of her friend's hand again, and this time they both moved away, slowly at first, but then faster and faster. In her heart, she knew it was hopeless too, but she didn't want to say goodbye to another friend just yet. She knew the time wasn't that far away, but it wasn't now, and for the time being that would have to be enough of a reason to keep them both going.

38

They carried on sprinting for several minutes until the landscape started to look a little more familiar. The shouts of the hunters diminished, but every now and again they caught the odd, "Over there," or "Here," drifting on the breeze.

The two women were heartbroken, petrified and fast running out of reasons to carry on their journey. Every step they took was a risk. Every time they stopped or slowed down was a risk. It was lose/lose, whatever they did.

"The cave," Lauren said.

"What?"

"This looks like the track to the cave."

They stopped. "You mean all this time we've been travelling and we're right back to where we started?"

"Looks like it."

They began running again, following the trail until they reached the sprawling spiny thicket that hid the entrance to the hiding place that Gabby had shown them. Lauren's legs had only just stopped bleeding, and heading back through would almost certainly open the wounds up and cause new ones, but they were out of options. She forced her way through as quickly as she could; Sal followed, repositioning branches where appropriate, doing her level best to make the chaotic jumble look untouched by human hands … or feet.

A moment later, their backs were propped up against the cold wall of the rock enclosure. Their swords and the small black pouch were at their feet, and their heads were in their hands. Both women sobbed hopelessly, not for themselves but for their friends, more specifically, their friend, Suzie. Neither of them had ever felt so hopeless, so ready to give up, and for her to sacrifice her life in a vain attempt to save them made the guilt unbearable.

Gradually, the tears subsided a little and Sal stared down at Lauren's legs. In the shadowy light of the cave, the thin bloody streaks looked like black lace stockings covering every centimetre of her bare skin. "Oh man, you really chose the wrong outfit, didn't you?"

Lauren didn't say anything at first, but then she almost blurted, "I love you, Sal."

"Love you too."

"I thought we were going to grow old together. I thought our kids would grow up together. I thought we'd go on family holidays together. I thought—"

Sal sidled up to her, putting a sisterly arm around her bare shoulders. Lauren grasped her friend's hand, and they remained frozen there for several minutes. The shouts of the men got louder and louder until they could hear them no more than a few metres away from the dense crop of thorny bushes that hid the cave's entrance.

"Just close your eyes," Sal whispered. "Close your eyes and it will be all over soon enough."

The voices of the men started to drift in the other direction. Even though Sal had taken precautions, she felt convinced that they'd be captured. She wasn't sure if it was good luck or bad luck that they weren't, but for the time being the black walls of the cave gave them a little respite from the chase if nothing else.

Lauren climbed to her feet and picked up her sword. "I think maybe what Suzie did wasn't such a bad idea. We're never going to get out of here … wherever here is. But we can do this on our own terms rather than theirs. My biggest fear right now isn't dying, it's dying alone. I don't want something to happen to you for me to be left alone or vice versa." She lifted the sword up in front of her. "It would probably be all over before we even knew about it."

Sal rose too. She grabbed her weapon and stood opposite her friend. They embraced each other tightly; seconds passed into a minute, then they finally broke apart. They regarded each other a little longer; then Sal looked down at her sword once more, turning it in her hand, gauging the weight studiously. "No."

"No what?"

"No. This isn't how it's meant to be."

"It may not be how it's meant to be, Sal, but it's how it is."

"No! No, no, no, no, no!"

Sal's eyes suddenly seemed wild as she stared across to her friend.

"Sal, What are you—"

"I didn't go through everything I've been through to go out without a fight."

"We've put up an amazing fight. Hell, you and I have—"

"No. I mean a proper fight. They want to kill us, then, by all means, let them try. I'm not going to make it easy for them, and by the end of today, I'm going to make sure that at least a couple more of these bastards wish they had never laid eyes on me. For Gabby, for Amber, for Pippa, for Suzie. I'm not going to feel sorry for myself anymore. I'm not going to be a victim. I'm not going to let them reduce us to making a suicide pact. I've fought all my life, and I'm not going to fucking stop now, and you know what? I'm not going to let you stop either."

39

A nervous smile crept onto Lauren's face, and she stared at her friend for a few seconds before speaking. "You're serious? You want to go out there and take these guys on?"

"What have we got to lose? We were just talking about killing ourselves for fuck's sake. Let's take a couple of these twats with us."

Lauren could see her friend becoming angrier by the second. "I … I don't know how."

"Yes, you do. You're not that little kid in school anymore who I always had to protect. You're fucking amazing, Lauren. You've done better than any of us. You've got a brilliant job; while I'm stuck behind a fucking perfume counter, you're an office manager. You play league softball; you're a really great artist; you can pretty much do whatever you set your mind to. I really don't understand how someone like you doesn't have more confidence."

"You were the one who told me to apply for the job. You were the one who went to tryouts for the team with me, you—"

"Yeah, but you were the one who got the job. You were the one who got in the team, and you know what? I told you that you could do those things and I'm telling you that we can do this. If we do nothing else before we die, let's give these guys a really, really bad day, if not for us then for our friends."

Their eyes remained fixed on each other for a few more seconds, and Lauren wasn't as unsure anymore. Sal was right. They didn't have anything to lose. "Okay."

"Don't worry, I'm not going anywhere. We're going to be together to the end."

Sal bent down, picked up the pouch, and attached it to her leather belt, and the pair of them went to stand in the mouth of the cave. They gazed up the embankment to the thicket; beyond it lay almost certain death, but at least this way it would be death with some kind of purpose.

"So, what's the plan exactly?"

"Avoiding being murdered for as long as possible."

"I'm glad you told me, I'd have looked a real fool otherwise. Seriously, what do we do? Where do we go?"

"Well, those two we heard went off in that

direction," Sal said, pointing to the right. "I say we go after them."

Lauren let out an anxious laugh. "We're really doing this, aren't we?"

"Yep, we're really doing this."

"It's mad … you do realise that, don't you? You've gone barking mad."

Sal smiled. "We all go a little mad sometimes."

"Err … quoting Norman Bates doesn't really help to put my mind at ease."

"Sorry, couldn't resist it. Right, let's do this." Sal walked up the incline and immediately began sweeping the sword from side to side, hacking and flattening the thorny growth as if she was an explorer in the jungle.

"What the hell are you doing? They're going to know we were here."

"You're still not getting it, are you? It doesn't matter. There's no more hiding. Not for them and not for us."

40

Lauren was grateful for not having to endure the same pain that she had on the way into the wild growth of bushes, but as she stepped out of the other side, she felt naked. She had no time to acclimatise to the strangeness of the feeling, however, as Sal immediately began running. She took a deep breath and followed her.

They carried on for several minutes before Lauren reached out and grabbed her friend's shoulder. "This is useless."

"What do you mean?" Sal asked.

"They could have gone off in a hundred different directions. We could be running around all day doing nothing but wearing ourselves out."

Sal sighed. "I suppose you're right."

"Hey. I've got an idea," Lauren said as a small smile appeared on her face.

"What?"

"We get them to come to us."

"And how do we do that exactly?"

"We need to go back to the cave."

"I told you, no more hiding."

"We won't be hiding. We're going to set a trap."

***

They almost stopped in mid-stride as the words "Sal, help me," shrieked through the forest. It came from behind them. There should have been no way that was possible, and the fact that one of their quarry was screaming did not bode well.

"Fuck it," said the larger man carrying the mace.

They both started sprinting back in the direction they had heard the sound. "This is shit. By the time we get there, it'll all be over."

"We don't know that. It might not be another team, they could have fallen in one of the traps; hell, they could be fucking scared of spiders for all we know. Just keep your eyes open."

The scream came again, this time followed by an agonised cry. "Damn it, I'm telling you someone else has got to them."

"They better not have done. I'm fucking sick of these rich weekend warriors wanting to take part in these. It shouldn't be fucking allowed. We need that bounty, that's our fucking bread and butter. All they're out for is a quick thrill."

"Danny, your fucking mic's on. Keep schtum."

"I don't fucking care. It's about time somebody said something."

"Look, let's talk about this later."

They slowed as they reached a familiar looking trail, but it was not the trail they slowed down for. Glistening in the peeking rays of the afternoon sun were two bloody throwing stars about a metre apart. "Keep them peeled, Scouse," Danny said, tightening his grip around the shaft of the mace.

"I'm telling you, we're too fucking late," he replied, raising his crossbow and scanning the entire area for movement. "I bet you anything Kemp and Brookes have beaten us to it."

"Less talking, more looking." The pair carried on walking until they reached a sprawling mass of bushes. A path had been beaten through, and a small piece of torn fabric hung on one of the thorny branches still protruding from the dense growth.

Scouse and Danny paused and glanced around. "What do you reckon?" Scouse asked, keeping his crossbow raised and ready.

"I think this might be our lucky day. I think one of the others got a couple of hits with the throwing stars, the girls lost them, and they beat a path through here."

"What makes you so sure they got away?"

"Well, if they didn't, I'm pretty certain there'd be some cunt doing a victory lap. Two girls, that's a hundred and fifty grand."

"Fair point," Scouse replied.

"Right, let's do this," Danny said. "You first."

Scouse started through the already hacked and chopped path, and Danny followed. Two of the hunters who had died earlier had been guests, happy to pay the buy-in price to experience the thrill of the hunt. Danny and Scouse were regulars, hired by the game organisers ... well, hired was the wrong word, invited by the game organisers. They did not get paid unless they claimed a scalp, and considering there were only two left, everything came down to this. "I think I see something ... it looks like a cave," Scouse said as they reached the halfway point.

"There are all sorts on this fucking island. It was ex M.O.D. Wouldn't surprise me if there were caves, tunnels—

" There was a sound of rustling bushes and a sudden blur to Danny's right, and that was the last thing that ran through his mind other than the blade that cracked open his skull lopping the top of his head clean off.

The whoosh and loud crack all happened in a heartbeat. Scouse spun around with his crossbow still raised, ready for action as always, but before he could so much as aim, a second glinting sword carved through the air towards him. The split second that it made contact with the bridge of his nose he instinctively pulled the trigger, but the bolt flew off into nothingness. There was not enough time to process the pain as the sword first blinded him then chopped through bone and brain. He collapsed as quickly as his partner, and in no time it was all over.

41

Sal and Lauren looked at each other. They were still in their respective battle poses. Blood dripped from their weapons, and despite the burst of activity being brief, they were both panting heavily.

The sharp thorns had cut their bare skin to shreds, but it didn't matter, they had won this first fight. "What … what should we do now?" Lauren asked.

"Get out of these prickles for a start."

They trudged through the bushes to the two dead figures. Sal reached down and picked up the mace one of the men had been carrying, and a menacing smile appeared on her face. She flung the sword into the thicket. "What are you doing?" Lauren asked as the katana blade disappeared.

Sal raised the spiked metal ball on a shaft in front of her. "This is definitely more me." She looked around for a moment, weighing their options. "Let's take cover over there. If there were any of the others in the area, they'll probably be coming to investigate."

The two women headed across to another leafy growth of bushes and crouched down behind it. "Did you hear them?" Lauren asked. "Did you hear what they said?"

"About us being on an island? Yeah."

"I know geography wasn't my strongest subject, but I don't remember reading about any islands off the Blackpool or Southport coasts, do you?"

"No."

"So, where the hell are we?"

"I don't know, Lauren. I really don't."

They stayed hidden for at least twenty minutes, occasionally popping their heads up to see if there was any movement, but there wasn't.

"Wherever the rest of them were, it looks like they were out of earshot," Lauren said.

"I suppose we'd better be—" A sudden sound made them both duck back down.

"Wait," said the deep, husky voice. "Look!" Obviously someone of few words.

"Looks like we're in the chase at last." It was a woman's voice, an American at that.

Lauren and Sal looked at one another with furrowed brows. "What the hell is this?" Sal whispered. Lauren just shook her head.

"Are they dead?" asked the American woman.

"Dead or very, very sleepy," the deep voice replied.

"If I wanted humour I'd have hired Chris Rock; now tell me, are they dead?"

Sal and Lauren heard rustling and cautiously angled their heads to peer over the bushes. The woman standing back from the thicket. She held an unloaded crossbow in her left hand. The giant of a man was heading along the beaten path through the bushes towards the cave. They both had their backs to Sal and Lauren.

"What should we do?" Lauren whispered.

"We should attack."

"Are you serious? Have you seen the size of that

guy?"

"Now," Sal hissed, and before Lauren could protest or even try to reason with her, the campaign had begun.

42

Sal realised her mistake a fraction of a second too late. She did not run wide enough of the bushes that had shielded them, and they flicked back creating a sound louder than any creature of the forest could make. The woman was not the issue, it would take her valuable seconds to load and aim her weapon, but the giant would be more than prepared for the assault. *Fuck!*

She emerged into the open, instantly causing the heads of the two hunters to turn in her direction. Their eyes glaring towards her through the gaps in the ski masks made a shiver run down her spine. The American began to fumble with her crossbow, and the giant immediately started out of the thicket.

The woman brought her crossbow up much quicker than Sal thought possible. She cocked it and placed the bolt in position. *Holy shit, I'm screwed.* Sal did the only thing she could think of doing, she flung the mace with every ounce of energy and strength she had. The weighty chunk of solid metal cartwheeled through the air towards its target. For a second, the woman was stuck to the spot like a deer caught in headlights. Then, at the last second, she ducked to her left.

"Aaaggghhh!" She moved just in time to avoid a fatal wound but not soon enough to avoid paralysing pain; the spiked ball smashed against her right cheekbone, ripped off the balaclava curtain and surrounding flesh, then tore through her ear. As it continued through the air, bloody morsels flew to the ground and the wounded woman's howl scythed through the forest. She dropped the crossbow, pushing both hands up to her mutilated ear. "Nooo!" she screamed again as the weapon clattered to the ground. She soon followed it, the torturous suffering rendering her immobile.

The sense of victory that Sal experienced evaporated instantly as the giant charged at her. "Fuck!" she muttered under her breath. Unarmed, out in the open, the colossal out-of-control bullet train raced through the thicket. It was her turn to be frozen to the spot now. *Who am I kidding? A couple of lucky thrusts with a sword, a decent throw with the mace that doesn't make me fucking Conan the Barbarian. Oh well, at least we chalked up another two for you, Suze.* Finally, she came to her senses and started backing away.

"Aaarrggghhh!" A female cry, Lauren's cry. She stormed past Sal, her sword pointing toward her target, homing in on him.

Sal stopped her retreat, suddenly transfixed like a rubbernecker on a motorway viewing a pile-up. Part of her wanted to reach out and stop her friend; part of her knew it didn't matter. This was all over one way or the other; the giant could probably take a dozen swords in the gut without even slowing down. They headed straight at one another on a collision course. The big man thrust his sword towards his attacker, and suddenly time stopped.

Lauren's eyes widened as she immediately realised that the giant's reach outmeasured hers by a good foot at least. The blade moved like a rocket veering towards her chest. Too late to dive left or right, she dropped to her knees, feeling the air part above her head. It was more her opponent's momentum than her own strength that drove her blade deep into his thigh. He let out an angry growl of pain but somehow remained upright. "You little bitch," he yelled, swiping low with his left hand and making contact with the side of her head. There was an echoing smack as she collapsed sideways to the ground with a surprised yelp and the sword came back out of her victim's leg issuing a fountain of blood. The giant dropped his own weapon, at once recognising the fact that his femoral artery had been cut.

The sight of Lauren brutally struck made a fresh fury swell inside Sal. She bolted towards the hulking figure, deliberately kicking the woman's crossbow out of reach as she went. She had no weapon but her own rage; however, that didn't stop her as she launched her assault. "Aaaggghhh!"

43

Sal leapt through the air like some mad rugby player executing a high tackle. She had no idea what she was doing other than playing interference. The giant was still clutching his leg, desperately trying to stop the bleeding, when he looked up to see the flying lunatic zeroing in. He straightened up, releasing his wound, and immediately, a torrent of blood spurted. He swung out batting Sal like she was some bothersome insect. She veered off course and went crashing to the ground, managing to roll a few times to lessen the severity of the impact.

The giant ripped off his belt, wrapping it tightly above his wound to form a tourniquet. Lauren gathered herself and dived towards her sword. Sensing the danger, the giant reached down to pick up his own weapon. Still on her knees, Lauren swung the blade round in a wide arc, hoping a wound on the opposite leg would make him stumble and then maybe, just maybe, she could finish him off.

Clang! The metallic vibration rang like a bell and sent a jolt like electricity through Lauren's arm, causing her to lose her grip. The samurai blade fell from her hand, and the giant brought his own weapon around and up, ready to finish off the cowering figure in one swift strike.

"Help … me," cried the American woman

pathetically, still holding both her hands up to her head.

Her anguished plea diverted the giant's attention for no more than a fraction of a second, but Sal was already closing in for her next attack. She dived again, not so high this time. He had no idea it was coming, and as her shoulder blade dug into the open wound, it felt like sandpaper grating against every raw nerve ending in his body. "Argh!" This time, he could not stay upright as she locked her arms around both of his massive legs. He collapsed like a demolished building, making the ground shake around him.

Sal jumped up again straight away, almost limboing as the wounded figure whisked his sword in her general direction from his prone position. He began to gather himself once more, but so did Lauren. She lunged for her weapon, immediately thrusting it towards the man, hoping she could in some way encumber him before he climbed back to his feet.

"Fucker!" Sal yelled at the exact same moment as she dived on top of him. He crashed back down, and Lauren's sword penetrated the side of his stomach.

"Aaaggghhh!" he screamed. Sal's face was just inches from his. His eyes fired death rays at her from behind his black polyester mask. She was doing her best to pin him and his hands, but she knew it was futile. Her only hope was that Lauren would make a kill strike sooner rather than later. "Ugh!" he grunted loudly, somehow managing to throw Sal off him, despite the wounds to his stomach and leg.

Lauren scrambled forward frantically trying to plunge the blade in further, but, inexplicably, the giant now had his banana-like fingers wrapped around the sword, halting any progress. His strength was unbelievable, almost superhuman, and despite his injuries, he managed to whip his own weapon around once more. Lauren saw the stainless steel flash in the air just in time to withdraw her blade once again and roll from its path. She felt the wind against her face as it crashed down, and displaced earth powdered her face.

The wounded figure turned onto his good side and struggled to his knees, eventually staggering to his feet. He paused for a second. Sal had retreated to grab her weapon, but Lauren was still on the ground. Anticipating the attack from the woman gathering her mace, the man mountain stamped down on Lauren's sword, pinning it to the earth, rendering it useless. Lauren tugged, but she was no King Arthur, and this was no Excalibur.

His own weapon was poised, ready to strike, and he cast a wild-eyed stare towards her. There was a horror behind those eyes that froze the blood in her veins. She let go of the grip and crab crawled backwards. Blood was still gushing from his side, but now the leg wound was not flowing so readily. Despite his injuries, he still looked like he could snap the pair of them in one hand.

The American woman continued cradling her wounds and sobbing as Sal stood not two feet away from her with the mace firmly in her grip once more. She and the giant locked eyes. One of them would have to make the first move. Sal toyed with the idea of threatening to kill the woman, but she had a sense that it would have no bearing on the big man's actions. She looked at his wounds. Any normal person would have been out for the count, in a coma from blood loss, but this was clearly no normal person. The seconds dragged on, and gradually Sal came to accept that no matter how much she willed it, she could not just make him fall down dead.

She took a step forward, and the man's grip immediately tightened around his sword. His eyes narrowed, and a menacing smile appeared on his face. He was not scared; he was not even nervous. He knew he was going to be the victor. Sal's stomach churned as she took another pace towards him. *What am I doing? Me and Lauren could just turn and run. Yeah, this prick would still be alive but we would too … for a while.* "Fuck it!" She began to charge, and the grin on her opponent's face broadened, almost as if relishing the challenge.

"Come on then, pretty. Let's have some fun." He sounded like some vile, mouth-breathing caricature and a ripple of revulsion ran through her as she moved in for the final melee.

"Aaarrrggghhh!"

44

Sal saw his massive biceps tense through the black material of the sweater. She didn't know if the blade would come from above, from the left, from the right, at a diagonal, or straight, but she knew that her only hope was to avoid it. If he made contact, he won. If he missed then … he could still win, but at least there was a chance, a slim chance maybe, but a chance that she could achieve a critical blow.

Something popped into her field of vision. At first, she mistook it for a small bird somewhere on the periphery of the stage of play, making its escape from the scene of unfolding carnage. Then she realised it wasn't a bird but a stone, a little smaller than the average computer mouse but roughly the same shape. It shot through the air towards the giant. It was only at the very last second that he saw it, but by then it was too late. He attempted to duck and turn at the same time, but the missile smashed against his temple. "Agghh!" he screamed, staggering to his left and dropping his head for a second.

A second was all Sal needed. She vaulted into the air, parrying the wavering sword with her arm and hammering the mace down over her shoulder. The spiked metal ball caved the giant's skull like a hammer bludgeoning an Easter egg. There was a loud crack followed by a spongy squelch as the weapon continued its journey into the brain. "Whaa!" Sal's momentum kept her going as the figure crumpled to the ground. She just managed to land on her feet, but her balance was gone, and she too crashed to the forest floor.

She lay there watching the huge figure as blood continued to gush around the shaft of the weapon protruding from his skull. She heard a retching sound and looked across to see Lauren, still on her hands and knees but vomiting as she witnessed the ghastly horror show.

Sal angled her head to look back at the American woman who was still sobbing weakly as she continued to cradle her wound. "My head … my head."

Sal gradually slowed her breathing and climbed to her feet. She walked over to the fallen man and bent down, taking a firm hold of the shaft of her weapon and pulling. The sound it made as it came out of the brain and broke through more pieces of bone made her feel sick to the stomach, and the sight of the grisly spiked ball caused her to throw up too. When she had finished, she wiped her mouth and headed across to Lauren.

"Are you okay?"

Lauren just looked up at her. "You didn't seriously just ask me that?"

"I mean physically."

Lauren put her hand up to the side of her face where she had been struck so violently. "I think I'm going to have a hell of a bruise, but no lasting damage."

Sal extended her hand, helping her friend to her feet. They embraced briefly before turning towards the woman.

"My head … my head," she kept saying softly between self-pitying cries.

"What are we going to do with her?" Lauren asked.

"Well, I don't know about you, but I've got an awful lot of questions that need answering."

They walked across to where the woman was curled up and stared at her for a moment. "More might be coming," Lauren said.

"Yep," Sal said, bending over and ripping the ski

mask from the woman's head.

"Aagh—Aaaggghhh!" The damage was worse than either Sal or Lauren had thought. The woman's cheek had been mangled, and as well as missing a chunk of ear, some of her skull was visible too.

Sal looked at the bloody balaclava in her hand then glared into the tiny camera. "Having fun are you, you sick fucks?" she said before scrunching it up and flinging it to the ground. She bent down again and roughly dragged the injured woman to her feet. "Get moving," she said, pushing her forward.

The woman kept on crying and continued to shield her ear, but she did as ordered. Lauren went to collect her sword and was about to follow when she stopped and took one final look around. *Three more bad guys down, one captured; that means there are only three left.* Suddenly, things didn't seem so impossible anymore.

45

They travelled for fifteen minutes. It was slow going, their prisoner stumbled more than walked, all the time repeating her cries of pain, not engaging with her two captors at all, almost as if she had mentally disconnected from the situation.

Lauren and Sal watched her and the surrounding landscape with equal suspicion. They knew there were more assassins out there somewhere. "Over there," Sal said, taking hold of the woman by the upper arm and forcing her to the left. There was no struggle; the woman just did as she was told. They went down a shallow embankment, and Sal pulled the huntress to a stop. "There, sit down on that trunk."

The woman did as ordered once more. "My head really hurts," she sobbed again. It was the first time she had addressed them since their journey had started.

Lauren took hold of Sal's arm and pulled her to one side out of earshot. "I know you want answers, but I really don't think we're going to get anything out of her. She's just constantly jabbering away to herself." They both looked back towards the woman, who remained oblivious to them. She was in her forties, with short, greying black hair. When half of her face and head wasn't caved in, she would have been quite attractive. Through the black top and jeans, it was clear that she had an athletic build. What she was doing in the midst of all this madness was baffling, but Sal was determined to find out what she could.

"Hey, hey," she said, snapping her fingers and gaining the woman's attention. The American's watery eyes looked up to Sal as she loomed over her.

"I need help," she sobbed.

"Yeah, no doubt. You answer my questions, and we'll get you help."

The woman looked at her. "You won't … you'll kill me."

"No. I'm sure if the positions were reversed, you'd kill me, but I don't get a kick out of murdering people. You're no threat to me; I've no reason to kill you."

"How will you get me help? You can't."

"Oh yeah? So if I went back to get one of those cameras, told them you needed help and started a nice big fire to send up some smoke signals, nobody would come?"

The woman thought for a moment as she rocked back and forth on the tree trunk. "How do I know you'll do it?"

Sal did her best to maintain eye contact, but her gaze kept being drawn away by the wounds on the woman's head. "I told you. I don't kill for fun, and if you don't get attention, I don't really rate your chances that much, so it would be the same thing as killing you myself."

"My head really hurts."

"I know … you've said … like fifty times. You

answer my questions, and we'll get you help."

"What questions?"

"What is all this?" Sal said, gesturing around.

The woman looked at her long and hard. "It's a game."

"A game? What are you talking about?"

"When you've hunted everything worth hunting on the planet, what's left?"

"So the ten of you are all just looking for a prize to have stuffed and put in your study?"

"It's a little more complicated."

"Well, you'd better uncomplicate it and make it quick."

"It's not just the hunting. There's a book open, a big book."

"What are you talking about, a book?" Lauren asked, puzzled.

"She means gambling … don't you?" Sal said.

The woman nodded and winced. "High-end gambling … millions of dollars. Who makes the first kill, who'll fall into a trap, how long the one in the rat pit will last … no one's ever escaped it. The odds on that are over two hundred to one. There are odds on how people will die—mace, bolt, arrow, sword … you get the drift. There is a team of hunters provided by the game masters, but up to six guest hunters can take part."

"That's you. You're a guest hunter," Sal said.

"Yeah … and that was my bodyguard you killed."

"So how much did it cost you?"

The woman pulled her hand away from her head and winced again as she saw it covered in blood. "Seven-fifty each."

"Seven hundred and fifty quid and you get to kill young women with impunity?" Lauren said disgustedly.

The woman looked towards Sal. "Your friend's not very bright, is she? Seven hundred and fifty thousand … seven hundred and fifty thousand each."

Lauren's mouth fell open a little. "So you … you paid one and a half million for you and your pal to hunt us down like animals?"

"Look. I've kept my end of the bargain, now—"

"I'm not done yet," Sal said. "This island, where is it?"

"I don't know."

"Bullshi—"

"They blindfold us. We fly into Glasgow Airport. We arrive at a rendezvous point at a specific time. They blindfold us, there's a car ride, then there's a helicopter ride. When we get here, the blindfolds come off."

"Are you telling me the only way off this fucking island is by helicopter?"

"You could always swim." There was half a smirk on her face, almost as if the frustration felt by Sal alleviated some of her pain. "Now, I need—"

"Why?"

"Why what?"

"If you've got all that money, you can obviously afford anything you want in life. Why this? Why would you want to kill innocent people for your entertainment?"

The woman snorted a laugh. "It's a feeling like no other in the world. It's something unequivocal. When you hunt an animal, you can sense their fear, you can almost reach out and touch their pain, but there is nothing like a human being kneeling down in front of you begging you for their life. I always make sure my first shot is never a kill shot."

"You're a monster."

"It's all a question of perspective."

"What do you mean?" Lauren asked.

"What do you think about fishing?"

"What?"

"A man who goes out in a boat and spends the

afternoon on a lake fishing. He catches a fish; it comes out of the water and suffocates. Is he a monster?"

"You can't compare the two."

"I am comparing the two. Is he a monster?"

"No," snapped Lauren. "Of course not."

"Why?"

"Because … it's just a fish. It's just a dumb creature … it's not important."

The smirk came back to the woman's face. "I told you, it's a matter of perspective. My personal wealth is close to four hundred million dollars. I employ thousands of people all over the world. I've had Hollywood stars and former presidents at some of my parties. To me you're just fish, you're not important."

Lauren raised her fist, but Sal stopped her. "What are you doing?" Lauren screamed.

"This isn't us. We're not like them."

"I think I've just been convinced otherwise," she said, trying to pull her arm free.

"NO!" Sal yelled, and suddenly Lauren backed off.

"What's wrong with you? You heard her. Our friends died for their entertainment. They murdered them for fun, nothing more."

"Yeah, and we're not going to kill someone to make us feel better. If our lives are in danger, that's a different matter."

"But—"

"But nothing, Lauren. It's not who we are." Sal turned towards the woman. "Stand up."

"You said—"

"I know what I fucking said, now stand up. We're heading back to where we left your friend. We need that camera, and it's just a waste of time me trailing there only to come back here, so get up and start walking."

"I can't believe you, Sal," Lauren said, looking at her sword, "I really can't believe you."

"I gave my word. She answered our questions, and

now it's time for me to keep up my end of the bargain."

"If it makes you feel any better, I didn't even have the chance to get a single bolt off today," the woman said, still with the insinuation of a smirk on her face.

Lauren shook with rage, and her clench tightened around the grip of her sword. "I hope you burn in hell."

47

Lauren did not talk to Sal on the return journey to the cave. All three of them walked in silence, but the huntress's footing seemed far more deliberate and stable now. The journey that had taken them fifteen minutes only took ten on the way back. Sal wondered how much of the pain had been an act to try to evoke sympathy. They came to a halt long before they reached the cave area. Sal carefully observed the treescape for several minutes.

"I thought this place would be swarming."

"Nobody is allowed to interfere with the field of play until the end," the woman replied.

"So, they're just going to leave you until it's all over."

"Yes."

"That's crap. She's lying. Not interfere with the field of play, what about that drone?" Lauren said.

"Remember, this is being … streamed. If there are lengthy periods of inactivity, the betting starts to suffer. One member of each team has a pager. The drone is a last resort but sometimes a necessary one."

They eventually broke cover. Sal and Lauren tensed as they marched towards the thicket, expecting to be rushed at any moment. They came to a stop just a few metres away from the woman's dead teammate.

"What now?" Lauren asked bitterly. "Are we going to give her a pedicure while she waits to get rescued?"

103

Sal looked at her friend. "You were in the Girl Guides, start a fire."

"Do you really think starting a fire in a forest is a good idea?" the woman asked.

"A little while back you were all for it," Sal replied.

"That's when I thought I was going to die. You could have burnt the whole place down for all I care."

"What then, we just leave you here with these weapons so you can come after us again?"

"I don't know if you've noticed, but my head's cut open and I've lost a lot of blood. I just want to get seen to."

"Take your jeans and top off."

"What?"

"You heard me. You want to get seen to, take your jeans and top off."

The woman frowned but, acknowledging that her captors held all the cards, did as she was asked. She handed them to Sal. "If you think I'm someone who can be easily humiliated, you're wrong."

"I don't give a fuck," Sal replied, throwing them over to Lauren.

"What do I do with these?" Lauren asked.

"Put them on."

"Err, no. I'd rather every centimetre of skin was torn from my legs than wear that bitch's clothes."

"Suit yourself, but you'll wish you had when night comes."

"I like your optimism," the woman said.

"I wasn't talking to you," Sal replied then turned to Lauren once again. "Tie her up."

"With what?"

"Belts, shoelaces, whatever."

Lauren walked over to the fallen giant and unhitched the belt from his leg then unthreaded his laces. She did the same with the other two dead men then bound the woman to a tree. "Anything else?" she asked angrily as she retrieved her sword.

"No." Sal walked across to the balaclava she had thrown down earlier and picked it up, focussing straight away on the camera. "Hey, fuckos," she said, angling the lens in every direction. "You recognise where this is?" She panned round to where the woman was tied. "You'd better come and get your meal ticket; otherwise the cheque might bounce. She's lost a lot of blood, so I wouldn't piss about. Of course, if that's considered interfering with the field of play, then that's too bad, but we've done our bit. Hope you all get fucking knob rot. Catch you later." She marched over to the woman and put the balaclava over her head the wrong way round.

"I suppose I should say thank you. I'd have finished me off."

"Yeah, well, so would I," Lauren said.

"I told you. We're not like you people," Sal replied. "Come on." She reached down, picked up the jeans and sweater that Lauren had flung to the ground, took hold of her friend's arm, and the two of them walked away. They turned back as they reached the edge of the small clearing. The woman had bowed her head, and her body was shaking. For all the bravado, she felt fear and pain just like them. They both secretly savoured her suffering for a moment before carrying on.

48

After a few metres, Sal stopped at the foot of a tree. She looked back in the direction of the tied-up woman. A variety of shrubs, bushes and saplings covered her from view. "This should do us."

"What are you talking about?" Lauren asked, still in an angry tone.

"You honestly think I'm going to let that bitch get away with anything? When they come for her, we'll trail them back to their base. How else do you think we're going to figure a way out of here?"

"A way out? You think we can get out?"

"Well, we've killed six, incapacitated another. We seem to be getting pretty good at this."

"Err … Sal. That last guy nearly obliterated both of us."

"Yeah, but he didn't, did he?"

Lauren thought about it for a while. "No… I suppose." She stared Sal in the eyes. "I was so angry with you. I thought you were going to let her go."

"Oh, like I'd let you in on the plan."

"What's that supposed to mean?"

"It means that you can't keep a secret to save your life. Name a year when you haven't been so excited about the birthday or Christmas present you've bought me that you haven't accidentally ended up blurting it."

Lauren was about to reply but then realised she couldn't. "I suppose you're right."

"You know I am. Now put these on," she said, handing her the jeans and the sweater.

"I don't want those things anywhere near me."

"Lauren, the evening isn't that far off, it's going to get cold. Your legs are cut to ribbons, you need to do everything you can to stay warm and protect yourself."

Her friend reluctantly took the jeans and slipped them on, pulling the black dress down over them as far as it would go. She then slid on the top. "How do I look?"

"Fucking lush," Sal said, and they both laughed.

"What now?"

"We climb the tree and keep watch."

"I could really do with a pee."

"Yeah, me too actually." They crossed to one of the bushes, undid their trousers and crouched down.

"Just like old times, when we used to go on long bike rides together, remember?"

Sal smiled. "Not quite like old times. I never

remember a bunch of psycho killers after us."

"Maybe not, but some of those shopkeepers were pretty pissed off when they caught us taking a whizz behind their rubbish bins."

Sal laughed. "Actually, you've got a point there. Remember that one woman who set her dog on us? Bloody hell, I don't think I've ever pedalled so fast in my life."

Lauren laughed and picked up her sword, looking at the bloodstained blade. "Do you really think we can get out of here?"

"I don't know. In all honesty, I really don't, but we haven't got anything to lose by trying, have we?"

49

They kept a silent vigil in the tree. There was a nook that they both managed to squeeze into, giving them a partial line of sight of the woman but enough cover to duck and hide if they needed to. The afternoon dragged on, and gradually the sun dipped further and further, giving way to the evening. They kept the huntress in constant sight, but no one appeared to collect her.

The evening gave way to night, a dark, moonless night. They did their best to keep watch, but the foliage blocked much of the meagre illumination the starlight offered, so it was really tough to keep their eyes on the almost naked figure. They huddled closer together and, eventually, despite their best efforts, drifted off to sleep.

It was Lauren who woke first the following morning. It took her a while to remember where she was and how she had got there. Sal's head was leaned in against her. They had their arms around each other for warmth and how they had managed to remain in that cosy nook without falling out of the tree was something of a miracle, but they were owed one at least.

Sal was nestled into her shoulder and still breathing heavily; hopefully she was having pleasant dreams. They would both need every little bit of comfort they could find to get them through the day ahead. Before drifting off to sleep, they'd had a whispered conversation about how strange it had been that no one had been to collect the multimillionaire huntress. Maybe these people really were that principled, or maybe the line she had fed them about who they were and what was going on was utter rubbish.

It took Lauren a few seconds to register as she peered through the leafy branches, but the American was gone. "Shit!"

Sal immediately stirred. "Huh? Wh … what? What's going on?"

Lauren held her friend a little tighter to make sure she didn't move suddenly and fall from their resting place. "She's gone, Sal."

"What?"

"The American … she's gone."

Sal blinked a few times, wiped her eyes and then sat up to look. "What the hell? How didn't we see them or hear them?"

"I don't know."

The two women carried on looking for a moment longer then reached behind to where they had left their weapons. "Come on. Let's go see."

They carefully climbed down from the tree and stayed low for a while, peering from behind an expansive growth of bushes, making sure that there were no hiding would-be assassins. When they were as sure as they could be that the coast was clear, they broke cover. Their eyes darted in every direction as they headed towards the tree where they had left the American.

They got there to find no sign of the woman or the restraints that had bound her to the tree. "What the hell?" Lauren said.

"What the hell?" Sal echoed her sentiment, but as

Lauren looked at her, she noticed her friend staring in a different direction. She followed Sal's gaze to the thicket. The giant and the other two men had vanished as well.

"How? How is that possible? I mean it was pitch black last night. We'd have seen torches or something if someone came. And it's not like one person could just drag away those bodies. You'd need a bloody forklift to shift that guy."

"What is going on here?" Sal's words had barely left her lips when the sound of a woman's panicked cry ripped through the morning air.

50

Sal and Lauren looked at one another then both started sprinting in the direction of the scream. As they got closer, it became apparent that there was now more than just one person screaming. They arrived at a clearing to see two women holding on to the legs of a third as she reached down into a pit. A fourth was frantically foraging in some nearby bushes.

"Oh shit. It's happening again," Sal said as she and Lauren looked on in disbelief. They ran forward just as the excited squeals of hundreds of rats rose into the air.

"Who the fuck are you?" screamed the woman in the nearby bushes.

"We'll explain later. Find a fucking branch, quick," Sal said, running towards the pit, while Lauren ran to help the woman forage. The young blonde screeched as the small, brown, furry beasts ran over her feet and up her legs. Sal looked down into her blue, already tear-filled eyes. "You're going to want to let go. Whatever happens, don't let go or your friend's dead."

The woman leaning over the edge started visibly shaking with fear. "I can't. I can't do it," she cried, wriggling

109

backwards, and jumping to her feet.

Sal planted her sword in the ground and dived towards the mouth of the pit where the other girl had been. She looked towards the two who had been holding her. "Grab hold of my legs, close your eyes and don't let go. And when I say pull, you'd better fucking pull."

"HELP ME!" the blonde girl pleaded as the foul-smelling rodents swarmed over her.

"Grab my hands," Sal ordered as her ribs banged against the ground. The girl reached up and wrapped her fingers around Sal's wrists. Sal did the same as a rat ran up the trapped woman's shoulder and over her face.

"Aaaggghhh!" It was a cry of torment. Sal had heard it before; she'd hoped she would never hear it again.

"Pull! PULL NOW!"

Sal felt the girl release her grip as rats became tangled in her golden hair. Her instinct was to bat them, to shun them away, but that instinct would result in certain death. For Sal, holding on to those wrists was like grappling with a couple of angry pythons. The girl wriggled and writhed and screamed and then it came … what she had been expecting all along. The first rats raced over her hands, up her arms and across her back. Sal stifled the urge to scream; she just closed her eyes and hoped the women pulling her would carry on pulling.

A split second later, she felt the grip release on her left leg. She dug the toe of her Doc into the ground as hard as she could, but it wasn't enough. Gradually, she started sliding, and the rats continued to run over her like a human bridge. More hysterical screams rose into the air. *Shit!*

51

Sal couldn't let go. What kind of person would that make her? As horrific as it was to feel the tiny pattering feet running up her arms, and across her back and legs, she refused to release her fingers. *If this is how I go, so be it.*

"What the fuck are you doing?" came the angry shout from Lauren as she frantically swept the back of her hand down Sal's leg, displacing the screeching rodents. Suddenly, Sal was no longer sliding; she and the young girl were being yanked out of the pit again in double-quick time. Within a matter of seconds, they were both rolling on the grass, feverishly batting the clinging rodents from their bodies. Lauren and one of the other young women were helping and, one by one, the rats dissipated, scarpering in a dozen different directions.

Sal climbed to her feet, and Lauren rushed towards her, immediately examining her bare skin for bites and scratches. Other than a few grazes, she was relatively unblemished, but as they looked down to the young woman on the ground, it was a different matter. Her legs and torso were covered in blood where the rats had bitten and clawed. She remained on her back sobbing while one of her friends held her hand.

"I know this is a lot to take in," Sal said, "but we need to get moving, now."

"We're not going anywhere until we get some fucking answers. Who are you? Where the fuck are we? What are you doing with those fucking weapons?" It was the woman who had been foraging in the bushes for a branch who spoke.

"My name is Sal. This is Lauren. Yesterday, we woke up here just like you did this morning. We started the day with one of our friends dying in a pit just like that, and it gradually got worse. Now, if you don't want to end up in a pain you wouldn't believe, get your friend to her feet and come with us."

There was a pause; then the woman who had asked the questions rallied the others. She couldn't be sure of Sal's story, but as this stranger had just risked a gruesome death to help her friend, which was more than any of them had dared to, she was inclined to believe what she said rather than not.

Lauren grabbed her sword, Sal picked up her mace, and the pair of them led the group away from the pit that was still alive with the noise of hundreds of hungry rats. They took the most difficult, obstacle-filled route they could. The girl from the pit was still crying hysterically as two of her friends carried her along, wrapping her arms around their shoulders and holding her tightly around the waist.

"My name's Erin. I suppose we should be thanking you," said the woman from the bushes as they traversed a fallen tree trunk.

"Yeah, I'd hold on to your thanks for a little while yet," Sal replied.

They continued in silence for several more minutes then Sal stopped. "What is it?" Lauren asked.

Sal turned to look at the other women. "Right, hopefully, we'll have a few minutes before they track us."

"Who? What are you talking about?" Erin asked.

"Look. We caught one of them yesterday. She could have been selling us a line of bullshit, but I don't think so. This is all part of a sick game."

"A game?"

"Yeah. There were five of us … six actually. But that's another story. Anyway, there are these hunters. We managed to kill half a dozen of them and badly hurt another one." Sal held up her bloodstained mace. "They don't have guns. They use weapons like these, and bows and arrows."

"This doesn't make any sense. We were on a girl's night out and the next thing we know, we're here."

"Same thing. Exactly the same thing happened to us," Lauren said. "It doesn't change the fact, though, that this is real, and it's happening now."

"But why?" Erin asked.

"This woman, she said about how there was a ton of cash changing hands. High-stakes gambling, plus some of the hunters themselves pay big bucks just to take part. She'd paid one and a half million for her and her bodyguard. Oh yeah, and the best part is we have no idea where we are other than some island off the Scottish coast."

"Scotland? But we're from Liverpool."

"Tell me about it. One minute we're having a few drinks in a bar in the centre of Manchester, the next minute we're running for our lives through a forest in Scotland; but, honestly, the geography aspect of this is the last thing we should be worrying about right now."

"So, what should we be worrying about?"

"Staying alive long enough to be able to worry about the geography aspect of this."

52

Erin looked long and hard at Sal, then at Lauren, then over to her friends. "Sophie, Emily, Willow – Will – and Charlie," she said, pointing. They each looked up and nodded, other than Will, who was still crying and in shock from her ordeal in the pit.

"Trust me when I tell you that we know exactly how you feel. But you're doing better than we were. By this time yesterday, we'd already lost one friend, and it didn't take that long for us to lose the rest of them."

"So, what do we do?" asked Charlie, a tall, athletic looking woman with short black hair and oriental tattoos running up and down her arms. She had pierced eyebrows, and thick liner emphasised her dark brown eyes.

"We spent most of the day running yesterday. It got us nowhere, and it got our friends dead. There's only one way out of this." She raised the mace up in front of her face. "We fight." A smile appeared on Charlie's face. Sal's expression suddenly flared with anger. "You think this is funny," she asked, glaring and facing up to the taller and

113

slightly scary-looking woman.

Erin stepped in between them. "You have to forgive Charlie. You've just said her favourite words."

Sal's glare turned from the tall woman to Erin. "What are you on about?"

"Charlie's a kickboxer. She's won medals and all sorts of shit. Trust me; there is no better person to be out with when some prick thinks he can get fresh with you."

"Yeah, well, I don't know what you think this is, but it's not a fucking pub tour around Merseyside. I've come across plenty of creeps too, but they've never tried to attack me with swords … well, not that kind anyway," she said, nodding to the samurai blade Lauren was holding.

"Look, I'm sorry," Charlie said, stepping forward and guiding Erin out of the way. "I didn't mean to make light of this, but if you're telling me I'm going to get the chance to meet one of the twat-bastards that did that"—she pointed towards Will—"then fucking bring them on."

Sal raised her eyebrows. "I hope you get the chance for revenge before you get an arrow in your neck or a crossbow bolt in your back."

"Where did you get those weapons from?"

"Like I said, we managed to kill a few of them yesterday."

"Okay, but how did you kill them before you got those?"

"Luck played a big part. But we armed ourselves with big branches and stuff."

Charlie nodded. "Okay, that's a start." She turned to the others. "Grab some branches, the longer the better." Without hesitation, all apart from Will started scouring the ground. "Maybe we could borrow your sword and chip away at the end of them," she said, looking at Lauren, "y'know, turn them into spears."

"Err … yeah … sure." Lauren looked at Sal, and both of them raised an appreciative eyebrow.

"Maybe these would help too," Sal said, reaching

into the small black pouch on her belt and retrieving a pair of throwing knives.

Charlie took one. "Not really good for whittling, but I'm happy to hang on to them if you're not using them."

"Sure."

"You got anything else in there?"

"Just these," Sal replied, pulling out a small handful of the stainless steel martial arts stars.

Charlie smiled, took one and flicked her hand as if she was dealing a playing card. The star shot through the air like a bullet, appearing a split second later buried in the trunk of a tree. "I used to love these."

"Used to?"

"Yeah. You don't really see shurikens anymore … except in martial arts films."

Sal undid her belt and removed the pouch, handing it to Charlie. "Maybe you should look after all of these."

Within ten minutes, the branches had been sharpened into spears. Lauren had torn her dress into strips, and she helped Emily, the girl who had originally been lowered into the pit to retrieve her friend, patch Will up the best they could.

Will climbed to her feet. Sadness and bewilderment painted her face, but at least she was vertical, and if nothing else, the spear helped to keep her that way.

"So, what now?" Erin asked.

Sal looked at her, then to Charlie, then to Lauren. "Now we go hunting."

53

The group retraced their steps. As they approached the clearing with the rat pit in the centre of it, they slowed down.

"They'll definitely have been here. I just don't know

if any of them will still be around. Everybody, keep your eyes open," Sal said as they all took cover while they visually checked the area. There was no sign of anyone or anything out of place.

"What do you think we should do?" Lauren asked.

Sal was about to answer when the noise of splitting wood made her jump suddenly. Forty-eight hours before, she would not have been able to identify the signature sound of an arrow piercing tree bark, but now it was only too familiar. It was not until Will dropped her spear that Sal and Lauren realised where the sound had come from. They looked more closely and then they saw it. The flights of the arrow were sticking out from Will's shoulder-length hair. The head had flown straight through her neck, stapling her to the tree she had been hiding behind. Her nose and face were squashed up to the bark, and both arms fell to her sides.

Sal spun around like a top. Her eyes immediately zeroed in on the black-clad figure nocking another arrow. "They're behind us!" she yelled at the top of her voice.

The remaining women hurdled bushes and skirted around trees. "What now?" Erin asked in a panic.

Before Sal had the chance to answer, a pained shriek left Sophie's mouth. They all spun around to watch as she fell to the ground. Sal looked in the direction of the pit once more to see two figures lurking on the other side of the clearing. One was reloading a crossbow.

"Shit, there are two of them over there. It's a fucking ambush. Hit the deck."

"Shit! Shit! Shit! This is it. We're screwed," Lauren cried.

Erin locked eyes with Sal, desperately hoping that the more experienced woman would have an answer to their current predicament. The look of terror in Sal's gaze told her she didn't. Eventually, she broke her silence. "The longer we stay here, the more time it gives them to fortify their positions."

"You're not saying anything to boost my confidence about us escaping this," Erin replied.

"I don't know what to tell you. The second we raise our heads, they're going to fire … that's if they're not closing in on us right this minute."

"You said that you killed six of them yesterday and disabled another. That means there should just be three left," Charlie said, looking across to Sal.

"Well … yeah. I sup—"

Charlie sprang into a sprint like a one-hundred-metre medallist off the starting blocks. Almost instantly, an arrow launched in her direction, but she ducked and rolled; it was only as she jumped back to her feet that she noticed another figure in a ski mask closing in on her.

Sal raised her head to see what was happening. She ducked back down again at the exact same second that a bolt whizzed over her scalp from behind. "Come on," she said, and the others dived and hurdled whatever greenery was acting as their cover, changing positions once again and becoming invisible to the would-be assassins on the other side of the clearing.

The archer raised his bow once more and fired, but Charlie dodged and weaved a second time, avoiding the deadly missile as it flew just centimetres away from her head.

The other hunter was nearly upon her now. *Damn, didn't think this through properly.* He raised his weapon, a double-headed battle-axe. Charlie shot a glance back to the archer, who was plucking yet another arrow from his quiver.

No time to take care of both of them. "Shit!" The axe swung down.

54

Charlie pivoted and cannonballed into the axe man's lower legs, forcing him to abort the swing and sending him off balance. He toppled forward as Charlie's shoulder smashed his feet from beneath him.

The archer paused; the second she was back on her feet she was his. Cue old-fashioned cash register sounds – Ker-ching – seventy-five grand in the bank and it wasn't even ten o'clock in the morning. Not yet, not yet … yes, stand, yes, three, two—

The mace appeared out of nowhere. It was already too late when he caught the rapid movement out of the corner of his eye. He started to pull back in a hopeless attempt to avoid it, but the spiked metal ball honed in, demolishing the right side of his face beneath the balaclava and lodging there. He flew backwards, his head bashing loudly against the base of a tree. The pain was like nothing he had ever experienced, a thousand stabbing daggers, a thousand sledgehammer blows. He lay there unable to move. Blood filled the back of his throat as he tried to suck in air. *Help! HELP!* His brain told his mouth to scream the words, but his mouth and his vocal cords were unable to respond. He was broken, well and truly.

***

The axe man climbed to his feet, enraged by the tall girl's unsportsmanlike manoeuvre. His considerable muscles rippled beneath the clinging material of his black top as he brought the heavy weapon up once more. Charlie saw his eyes narrow and knew it was time to make her move. She skipped back, planted her left foot and arced her right one round in a swift single movement. The toe of her boot cracked against his chin, and a spinning glob of saliva left his surprised mouth as he staggered with the force of the impact.

He swung the axe down, but it was a reflex reaction and Charlie sidestepped the strike as the blade burrowed into the earth. The axe man shook his head in an attempt to revive himself from the after effects of the kick as he hoisted the blade out of the ground. Another kick, this time from the left, jarred his head in the opposite direction, and he lost his grip on the axe. It fell to the earth with a thud as he stumbled to the side and then back. He straightened his head once more, but now he was starting to see double.

One, two, three, four punches to the face in quick succession. Suddenly, he couldn't breathe beneath the balaclava as blood poured from his nose. He ripped the black mask off and stood there for a moment, wavering on his feet.

Charlie remained in fight pose with her fists raised and her legs perfectly poised. "There was a part of me that wanted to see what kind of utter twat face would do something like this, but now I have, I understand better than ever why you wear that mask, you ugly, fat, shrivel-dicked little wank stain."

He opened his mouth to say something, but one, two, three, four more punches sent him reeling, and he collapsed to the ground. Without a second thought, Charlie grabbed the axe and brought it up over her head. "Please."

"Aaarrrggghhh!" She brought the weapon down with such immense force that, even after it bisected the hunter's skull, one of the blades became completely buried in the ground. Blood sprayed over her face and arms as a self-satisfied smile curled the corners of her mouth. "That was for my friends." She reached down and hoisted the axe from the earth. The bloody tissue slopped from it onto the soil and leaves as she stepped to the side of the fallen figure. "And this is for me." She hammered the twin-headed axe down once more and savoured the feeling and the sound of it carving through her victim's neck. The already mutilated head rolled to one side like a misshaped football. "Fucker!"

55

The other women only just reached her as she made the final strike. They had been mindful of the two hunters on the other side of the pit, but it appeared for the time being they had chosen not to pursue them into the trees.

"Charlie … Charlie." It was Erin's voice and Erin's hand that gently touched the back of her friend's shoulder.

Charlie's head spun towards her. Fire was still burning in her eyes, but the flames died down as she realised this first battle was over. "They killed Will and Sophie."

"I know."

"Where's the other one?"

"Over there, Sal got him."

The whole troop marched across to find the lone figure curled into a foetal position with the mace sticking out of his head. How he was still alive no one was quite sure, but as he wept like a lost child, they all knew he was not long for this world. Charlie stepped forward with a menacing snarl fixed on her face. She brought the heavy axe up and took a deep breath.

"Wait!" Sal ordered.

Charlie's face reddened with anger as Sal's hand clutched her arm to stop her. "No."

"I said wait," Sal replied, stepping in between Charlie and the dying man.

Erin placed a calming hand on her friend's back once again, and Charlie lowered the weapon. Sal turned around to face the groaning figure. She reached down and carefully removed the camera from the small housing in the balaclava then dropped it on the ground and crushed it with the heel of her boot. "You answer my questions, and I'll make this quick for you. You don't, and I'll let Hannibal Lecter's crazier sister here have her fun. You understand me?"

His one remaining grey eye fixed on her. "Yes," he whispered in a laboured breath.

"I counted four of you. There should have only been three. How come there's an extra one?"

He looked confused for a moment; then he understood. This must be one of the girls from the previous

120

day. They had been told there were survivors. In the history of the competition it had never happened before and then, on two consecutive days, contestants … victims had survived. "New day. New teams."

"You mean there are ten of you?" No answer. Sal kicked his legs. "You mean there are ten of you?" she asked again.

"Yeah."

"So you flew in this morning?" No answer. "So you flew in this morning?"

"No."

"So, you were one of the ones from yesterday."

"No." His eyes were opening and closing now as if he was struggling to fight off sleep.

"What then? Fucking teleporter?"

"Boat."

Sal and Lauren shot shocked glances towards each other. "Boat?"

"Paying guests are flown in. We're shipped in."

"Where? Where's the boat?"

The man suddenly vomited, but Sal stifled the urge to be sick herself as she watched the blood infused, partially digested food dribble down his chin and over his clothes. "Please," he sobbed.

"Where is it?"

He sniffed loudly as more tears rolled from his eyes only to be soaked up by the material of his black mask. "East. East of the island."

"Okay … other than the hunters how many more people are on the island?"

He let out a long breath, and for a moment Sal didn't know if it was his last, but then he breathed in again. "Six … not on the island though … clean-up squad on the boat. That's it … nothing more to tell. Now please."

Sal and Lauren looked at each other again; then Sal reached down and took a firm hold of the mace's grip. She eased it out of the man's skull, and the cracking of bone fragments could just be made out over his agonised screams. She was grateful that he still wore the ski mask because the small amount of the injury that she could see made her stomach swim and churn. Lauren stepped forward and thrust her sword straight through the man's heart, putting him out of his misery once and for all.

Sal turned around. Emily was facing in the other direction gripping her wooden spear tightly and making sure the other two hunters did not appear, but Charlie and Erin both fixed her with their stares. "Boat or not, it doesn't really matter, does it?" Erin said. "You said it yourself, there's no way out of here."

"Yeah … that was then." Sal's eyes moved towards the axe Charlie clutched in her fist. "This is now."

56

Charlie and Erin looked at one another, neither understanding what Sal was talking about. Even Lauren looked confused. "Sal, what do you mean?" she asked quietly.

"The axe," she said, nodding to the hefty weapon Charlie was holding.

"What about it?"

"We could chop down one of the trees on the perimeter. If we do it right, it will smash straight through the fence, and we'll be able to get out of here … maybe find that boat."

"Holy shit!" Lauren blurted. "Do you think so? Do you really think we can do it?"

"Why not?"

"I'm all for optimism," Emily said, overhearing the conversation, "but it doesn't change the fact that there are another eight psychos out there somewhere looking to hunt us down and kill us."

"Well, yeah, there is that," Sal said.

"I like the idea," Charlie said. "So east … which way is east?"

"Jesus, Charlie. Even I know that," Erin replied. It was still fairly early, and although the sun had made its first appearance a while back, it was clear as to where it had risen from. She pointed. "That's the way we need to head."

They retreated further into the forest, away from the rat pit, before they changed their course to head towards the sun. They all walked side by side, in virtual silence. Their eyes searched through the shadows for movement. Occasionally Emily sobbed, as much from fear as from the sad loss of her two friends, but Erin and Charlie remained stoic. There would be time to mourn later, if and when they got out of this mess.

There was a loud crack from somewhere to the side of them, and they all ducked down.

"What the fuck was that?" Charlie asked.

"Stay calm," Sal replied.

"Oh yeah, like just saying stay calm is going to make me stay calm."

"One of the tricks they use is herding."

"Eh?"

"Herding. They try to get us all moving in the direction they want, straight towards one of their traps."

Emily started sobbing more consistently. "I'm scared."

Erin reached out and took her hand. "It's alright. We're all scared, but we're going to get out of this tog—"

There was another loud crack; this one was from the direction they'd been travelling in. A third sounded from the direction they had travelled from. Emily's sobbing became hysterical crying as fear consumed her. She stood up, shaking Erin's hand free.

"Get down," her friend hissed, but Emily turned and began to sprint south, the one clear direction that no sound had come from. An arrow shot towards her from somewhere in the trees, then a bolt. Each one missed her by a matter of inches. The other four women tentatively rose, all feeling the same fear but sharing the same gut instinct, that Emily was doing exactly what the hunters wanted her to.

She sped through the woodland as another arrow whistled by. Her eyes were foggy with tears, but she could still see enough to zigzag, stoop and dodge. She watched as a bolt chipped the bark from a tree up ahead then veered wildly off course. The tree had a small green cross painted on it – *weird* – but then again, what wasn't weird about this whole thing? She was doing it, she was escaping. She threw a quick look back to see if her friends were following, but they were just watching her, in a half crouch. *More fool them.*

Her foot landed on what felt like a springboard but wasn't. There was a sound … the kind of sound a tree makes when it falls … but not. Then the ground shifted before her. Earth, leaves and other woodland detritus flew in a hundred different directions as a grid housing dozens of sharp wooden stakes sprang like a mousetrap. It was already too late for Emily to do anything. She did not even have time to scream before the spikes penetrated her body. She was still conscious when the spring-loaded mechanism slammed her down onto her back and pegged her to the ground like an entire team of heavyweight wrestlers.

Emily could hear her breathing become more laboured. She could hear the blood collecting in her lungs. She could feel the pain of multiple wooden spikes stabbing into her all at the same time as the light slowly started to fade. The frame of the trap continued to pin her as fresh tears filled her eyes.

Bushes rustling … footsteps. *Is it Charlie and Erin coming to save me? Is there still a chance?*

"Fuck!" It was a man's voice. "That's another one we don't get paid for."

"No time to mope, the others are doing a fucking runner. Come on or we'll lose them."

The footsteps died away as the two men ran off. Emily needed to cough, but the pressure of the frame against her ribs was too great. She tried to suck in a breath of air, but all she inhaled was more blood. Her eyes widened, her face turned red, and then everything went black.

57

They could only see two of the women as they raced through the forest. Had another team already found their friends or had they made the foolish decision to split up? It didn't matter either way. They were heading towards a straight track, and as soon as they hit that, there would be enough time to aim and take them out.

What a day. It had only just begun and already one team was down—pros, not rich hobby hunters, and three gladiators, that's what they called them, and at the moment they were living up to their name.

This was the tenth hunt Rybald and Savage had been involved in. They had worked for their boss as muscle for twelve years, and the first two competitions had been a flat fee for taking part. After that, the stakes for success and failure had changed considerably. A good day could give them a nest egg. A bad day could put them in the hospital and out of action for a few weeks.

Both men withdrew arrows from their quivers ready. "I'll take the left, you take the right," said Rybald.

"Don't miss. There are only four left. If we—" The loud thump sounded like a sledgehammer hitting wet sand. As Savage flew backwards, he saw something sticking out of his chest. He followed the long handle to see a tall, muscular tattooed woman with a hate-filled grimace on her face. It was only then that his pain receptors kicked in.

He smashed down onto the ground with the axe still in his ribcage. His head smacked against a small sharp stone, sending another spasm of agony through him. Paralysed by his own suffering, he lay there knowing ... feeling his lifeforce leaving him. What was that? A shadow ... a crow? *Oh my God!* He felt the blood spatter against the material of his balaclava as his team mate's head spun down to the ground. It brushed his left arm as it landed, then bounced, finally coming to rest between his bicep and his ribs. He felt revulsion as the blood soaked his sweater sleeve, but there was nothing he could do about it. As much as he wanted to move, he couldn't.

The tall tattooed woman loomed over him with a bitter smile on her face. Then another figure appeared; she was wearing the same outfit he was, minus the mask. The blade of her sword dripped with blood fresh from the kill. A sound—not sure what. A second later, a glob of phlegmy spit covered his right eye.

"Fucking bullseye," Charlie said, smiling wider than ever now. "Go on, you try."

"Err ... no, you're okay," Lauren replied.

"Suit yourself." Charlie snorted and cajoled the muscles in the back of her throat and nose to create another phlegm bomb then spat again. "Phleugh!" They both watched as the thick swirl of liquid landed in the left eye of the dying man. Charlie balled her fist and victory punched the air. "Yes! Fucking double top."

Lauren cringed a little. *Gross!* "Come on; let's catch up with the others."

They both took one final look at the headless corpse and the dying man then Charlie reached down and heaved the axe blade from his chest with a stomach-turning slurp as blood and tissue rushed to fill the void that had been created by the blade.

The man watched through spit-distorted eyes as the figures disappeared out of view. Still he could not move; still the pain overwhelmed him. *Please let this end ... please.*

58

Varak Sarafian – the Rat, as he was often referred to – leaned back in his chair looking at the wall of monitors. The ones in the middle displayed the field of play from the point of view of the hunters, the various pits and booby traps, and occasionally the drone. Those were the images the subscribers saw … those who had a vested interest in the game. Officially, he knew none of them by name. All transactions were carried out through offshore accounts. Unofficially, he knew that a number of the patrons were among some of the wealthiest and most influential people on the planet. They gave millions, hundreds of millions, billions sometimes to charities—true philanthropists. But they also did this. They took part in the ultimate game. Maybe not actively … maybe they weren't the ones who donned the black outfits and ski masks, but they all revelled in the thrill of the hunt.

There were sixteen booby traps on the field of play. On any given day, any one of them could be sprung. Trap thirteen had just paid out, and immediately there had been a spike in betting on the others. These last two days had been unique. They had never had the prey lasting more than twelve hours, but it had been incredible for business. Sarafian had been doing this for sixteen years. He owned five islands like this dotted around the world, but this week had already surpassed the previous record, and it wasn't over yet.

The monitors to the left were for his and his team's eyes only. Dozens of tiny cameras placed strategically in trees and, most importantly, the dock told them what none of the others did. But they were for information and emergencies only. There was a code of play, an absolute right and an absolute wrong. The odds were already stacked against the hunted, but if they beat the system, fair play. It was up to the hunters to stop them.

The rich American cunt from the day before—she had deserved to die. But hats off to those two girls, they saw an opportunity to find a way out and tried to take it. It wasn't their fault, they didn't know the after-game procedure, that a group of 'cleaners' would move in with night vision goggles, stab vests and an armed guard to remove the day's fallen, to reset the traps, to repair whatever needed repairing.

The monitors on the right showed odds and current betting. And the one in the far bottom corner was for encrypted messages from the punters. This was the screen that he was now contemplating. He reached for another cigarette from the silver case that lay open on the table in front of him. He lit it, sucked and then released a plume of blue smoke into the dimly lit room. Two figures were busily tapping away on keyboards. This year, there were over three hundred participants in the world's most prestigious yet most secretive gambling event. Much of it was automated, but there was still a need for the personal touch.

Sarafian's fierce reputation ensured complete loyalty from his employees, but these two were loyal for a different reason. After his brother had passed away – the polite term for being kidnapped, beheaded, then partially dissolved in hydrofluoric acid – Sarafian and his wife had legally adopted Lilit and Hayk. One day, they would take over the reins of the family business. His nephew and niece were a formidable partnership. They were both intelligent, diligent and ruthless. The acquisition of wealth was like a religion to them, and Sarafian was their god.

Lilit suddenly turned around and stared at her uncle with a knowing smile. "What do you want me to do?" she asked, no hint of her family's native accent in her voice. One would expect not considering the price of her Ivy League education.

Sarafian smiled back. "I'm still thinking. Why the impatience?"

"You didn't just ask me that."

Sarafian's grin widened and he took another long drag on his cigarette. "Hayk, how many now?"

Hayk hit a key to refresh the screen. "Seven, Papa."

Sarafian exhaled deeply once again. "What do you think, my children?"

"I don't know, Papa," Hayk replied.

Sarafian's eyes travelled across to Lilit. "And you?"

"I say of course we should. It's seven now. If we do it, it will be ten, twenty, thirty times that figure in no time. Just because it has always been done a certain way, it is not sensible to close our mind to potential streams of income. We can still root for whomever we want, but to turn money away because of sentimental notions of loyalty shows weakness."

The grin vanished from Sarafian's face. Lilit had always tested the limits of what she could get away with. *Was this an open criticism of him or just more probing?* He looked from her to Hayk and back again then finally let out a breath. "This is history we are making today, my children. Open the book. From this point on, they can place bets on the hunters and the hunted to make the next kill."

59

Lilit and Hayk immediately got to work, and within the first minute Lilit's prediction came to fruition. The screens lit up with feverish betting taking place. The smile reappeared on Sarafian's face; then his eyes narrowed. "Lilit."

"Yes, Papa," she said, spinning around in her chair.

"Open another book on the gladiators."

"I don't understand."

"There are four of them. That's fifteen different permutations for survival. Any single one of them could get through, any two of them, any three of them, or all four of them. Let's see if the fish are biting."

Lilit beamed. "Yes, Papa."

***

Lauren and Charlie were out of breath by the time they caught up to their friends. "Okay, chalk up two more of the little twat bastards," Charlie said.

"I don't suppose they had anything better than this, did they?" Erin asked, holding up the sharpened branch.

"Sorry," Lauren replied. "They both had bows."

"Err … why are we still going in this direction?" Charlie asked. "I thought you said we needed to head east."

"We do," Sal replied.

"So why are we going this way?"

"'Cause whatever we seem to do, they're one step ahead of us. They had an ambush set up. We just lost three of your friends in like … minutes."

"Okay, but we got four of them."

"Yeah, obviously maths isn't your strong point. How long do you think we're going to last if that happens again?"

Charlie pulled Sal around to face her. "Don't get fucking funny with me, you sarky little bitch."

Sal sighed. "I'm sorry. But I'm getting sick of this shit. There are six of them left. If they make the next move, they might finish us off before we even know what's going on."

"So what's the answer?"

"I'm still working on that. Until then, let's keep our eyes open and hope to fuck we see them before they see us."

The four girls continued until they reached an embankment and were met with the familiar sound of running water. Sal and Lauren looked at one another. It was this stream that had carried them to the bridge and the fence the previous day. They all stopped and took a drink then sat on the rocks for a moment.

"Ha … I was meant to be starting a new job today," Erin said.

"Don't worry," Sal replied. "Just explain to them what happened. I'm sure they'll understand."

Erin laughed, then Charlie joined in, and before long all four of them were giggling. "Good one," Erin replied.

"Listen," Sal began, "I've been thinking. We don't want to kill all of them."

"Speak for yourself," Charlie said. "I want every last one of these bastards to bleed out, slowly."

"Yeah, eventually."

"What are you thinking, Sal?" Lauren asked.

"I'm thinking that if we kill the rest of them, some stuff might happen that we don't want to happen."

"Err … newsflash," Charlie replied, "that's already going on."

"Yeah, but think about it. If this is a game and the last camera feed goes dead, then that's game over, isn't it? When that happens, they might send in another ten hunters, and we could be back to square one, or they might send the boat away … or I don't know what. But my point is we need to be clever about this."

Charlie and Erin looked at one another. "That's actually pretty smart," Erin replied.

"Well, don't go congratulating me just yet. At the very least we could do with evening up these odds a little if we stand any chance of getting out of here alive."

"Any thoughts on how to do that?"

"One. But it's a long shot."

"Define long shot," Charlie said.

"It could bring all of them down on us at the same time and turn into a bloodbath that makes everything that's gone before look like a Sunday afternoon picnic in the park."

Charlie smiled. "I like the sound of it already."

60

Sal and Lauren led the way back to the rat pit. They looked towards it to see the creatures were still squealing and screeching wildly, and as the women peered down, they each stifled the urge to vomit.

"So, this is it? This is your plan?" Erin said.

"I didn't say it was great," Sal replied.

"No, you didn't, which I suppose is just as well."

The four women looked at one another nervously, all knowing what decision came next but none of them wanting to raise it first.

"It's my idea, I'll do it," Sal blurted.

"No. I don't want you to," Lauren replied.

"Nobody wants to, but somebody's got to."

"Look, I'll do it," Charlie said.

"Definitely not," Sal replied.

Charlie took a step towards Sal and glared down at her. "And why definitely not me? What problem have you got with me doing it?"

"Well, apart from clearly being some kind of fucking psychopath, you're the best fighter we've got, and I'd really like you doing the fighting rather than being the bait."

The anger left Charlie's face and was replaced by a wide grin. "That's fair enough, I suppose."

Sal smiled too. "We've all got to play to our strengths."

Lauren sunk her sword into the earth and threw her arms around her friend. "Be careful."

"You too. Nobody's got an easy ride on this one." Their embrace finally broke, and Lauren collected her sword. "Love you, Sal."

"Yeah, love you too."

There was sadness in both their voices. This half-baked plan was a real Hail Mary, but they had to try something or risk getting picked off one by one. Charlie handed Sal one of the throwing knives and nodded respectfully. Sal took it and watched as it glinted in the morning sun as the other three women disappeared into the surrounding greenery.

Sal remained there, her nose twitching as the smell of the pit seemed to get stronger by the second. She turned a full circle. There was no sign of her friends now. If she couldn't see them, hopefully there was no chance the hunters would either.

Sal placed her mace on the ground and lifted her once white T-shirt. Her body was bruised and battered, but she had become numb to the pain after the trials of the previous twenty-four hours. She knew, however, that she would not be numb to what came next.

"Aaaggghhh! Aaaggghhh! Lauren! Aaaggghhh!" The screams rose up through the trees, scaring hundreds of birds into flight. The knife cut through the fat on the small amount of flab on the side of her belly that she had promised herself she would get rid of ever since Christmas. The wound was not too deep, but it had the desired effect. She pulled her T-shirt back down, and the blood immediately began to pool bright red against the thick cotton. She fell to her knees and onto her front. Then she waited.

She and Lauren had seen the hunters operate numerous times. They were always in pairs, but sometimes the pairs joined others. Hopefully, her screams would not be detected by all three remaining teams at once because then the game really would be over.

61

Sarafian continued smiling as the betting screens refreshed, but only part of it was down to the vast figures that were being transacted. "I really like these girls," he said.

Lilit and Hayk swivelled around in their chairs. "You should offer them jobs," Lilit said, only half joking.

"Lilit, my dear, you don't get to where I am by not being a good judge of people. If any of these girls ever met me, they would try to kill me. Failing that, they would blow the whistle on our entire enterprise, but, nevertheless, I like them. I like their spirit, their ingenuity. They are warriors, Amazonians. If they win … and they deserve to win, they should be celebrated. They deserve that."

Hayk and Lilit looked at one another with confused expressions then turned back towards Sarafian. "What are you saying, Papa?"

"The house. Instruct the captain and his men to prepare the house for them."

"We have never used the house," Hayk said.

"Were you not listening? These girls are special. If they are the victors, they deserve something equally special."

"Yes, Papa," Hayk replied, grabbing a burner phone and dialling a number he had written on his hand.

***

Sal lay there, her cheek against the earth and her eyes closed. *A voice … no, voices plural. This is it. Shit! Didn't take them long to get here, they must have been close by. I can hear them on the perimeter. They're surveying the scene. Do they think it's a trap? Is this all over before it's begun? Whatever happens, I can't screw this up.*

One minute ran into two then three. More voices. *How many exactly? Was it four or six? Shit! This is bad.*

Footsteps. *Sounds like just one person … testing the ground. This is bad—really, really bad. Fuck! He just nudged the mace away from my hand. OWW! This fucker's going to pay for kicking me in the ribs. Can't move … expected this. Just hope he doesn't fire a bolt into my head. What's he doing? Is he just looking around or has he seen something?*

"Well?" asked a gruff voice from somewhere near the edge of the small clearing.

"I'll tell you when I know."

"Oh yeah, take all the time in the world, it's not like we're doing anything else, is it?"

"Fuck you."

"The pair of you, fucking button it," said a different voice this time.

A long, long pause then a presence. *He's kneeling beside me. What's he doing? Fingers on my neck. Shit, the game's up. The plan's gone to shit. We're fucked.*

"There's a pulse. It's crazy fast."

"Well, don't fuck about, finish her off and let's move on," the gruff voice replied.

Sal heard the sound of a knife been withdrawn from a sheath. This was it. If she didn't act now, she was dead. Her eyes flicked open, and she rolled hard and fast, immediately wrapping her arm around the back of the hunter's legs and tripping him.

He fell forwards with a short, surprised cry and landed heavily on his stomach, dropping his bow. His head smashed down just inches away from the edge of the rat pit.

"Aaarrrggghhh!" A woman's battle yawp boomed from where Sal had heard the voices of the other men. She shot a glance across to see the glinting axe blade carving through the air towards someone … something out of her view. A split second later, there was another scream, but this was of a different type. A hunter sprang to his feet. He was missing an arm and blood was gushing as he stumbled back over the bush he had been using for cover.

Sal's mouth dropped open in shock as all thoughts of a crafty escape disappeared in a heartbeat. *We're in it now.*

62

Sal reached for her mace and sprang to her feet as another cry erupted from the perimeter. She couldn't see what had caused it, but it sounded like a man's scream. Almost immediately, a bolt flew in her general direction. It was not a well-aimed shot, and it was past her in a split second. The crossbow it had come from skidded across the ground as Erin came into view. Whoever owned the weapon had bigger problems than Sal right now.

A grunt, and suddenly Sal was crashing back to the ground. The hunter who had approached her was back in the game. Before she could gather herself, the searing pain of a knife blade entering her leg made her howl. Impulsively, she swiped the mace in her attacker's general direction, making heavy contact with his arm.

"Fucking bitch!" The metal spikes ripped at his bicep, forcing him to release the grip of the knife but not without twisting it a little in the process. Another jolt of agony raced through Sal, igniting the spark of a memory. She was thirteen, and her mother had broken a record by being with the same lowlife for about a month. Sal and he had been alone in the cramped council flat, and he'd been drinking. He'd tried to make a move on her, and she'd fought him off, but as she ran back to her bedroom to barricade herself in, he'd flung an ashtray at her, hitting her hard on the back of the head. Up until now, that had been the worst pain she had ever endured, but this was on a different level.

The combination of hatred and adrenaline consumed Sal, and she struggled to her feet with the knife still in her leg. She pulled it out, throwing it to the ground angrily, ignoring the pain and the pulsing blood for the time being. Her assailant sprang to his feet too, but now he was weaponless. His bow lay on the ground a few feet away, but experience told him tackling the woman and retrieving the knife was his best chance for success. After all, she was just a girl, he would easily be able to overpower her, weapon or not.

There were another two screams from the tree line, but Sal couldn't look now. Everything came down to this one moment, as predator and prey weighed each other up, waiting for the other to make the first move. Sal tightened her grip around the mace, the pain in her leg forgotten for the time being.

Another scream. *Oh shit! That was Lauren!* Sal couldn't help it. Fear for her friend involuntarily drew her gaze to the tree line for just a split second, but that was all the hunter needed. She knew it was a mistake as she was doing it. She could almost feel the air move around her as he pounced. Lauren's sword had been knocked from her hand by a broad figure sporting an almost identical blade. *Shit!* Anger surged through Sal like a torrent; her muscles flexed and she swiped with all the power she could muster.

There was an echoing crack as the mace connected with the side of her attacker's head. He veered off wildly, barely managing to stay on his feet as the shuddering vibrations of the impact ran through him, and then something else happened … something he didn't think would ever be possible.

63

He had been a part of this game since the beginning. Sixteen years and the worst injury he'd ever suffered was when a bowstring had snapped and lacerated his cheek. He never thought this could be possible, not this. His right foot didn't hit the ground, it just kept dropping lower and lower, it was too late to try to pivot or dive, the momentum was all downward. Up until this point, his problem sinuses had blocked out the foul shit-smelling rodents as they jostled and vied for position in the pit, desperately trying but always failing to scale the greased walls.

Instinctively he dropped the knife and spread his arms out wide like wings in the vain hope that he could grab on to something that would halt his fall. His left leg reached maximum bend and twisted as he toppled. He became deaf to the shouts and cries from his fellow hunters and the other women as he fell. All he could hear was the feverish chattering, squealing, hissing sounds of the rats that had been deliberately starved for this game. Granted, the strong would have fed on the weak, subduing their hunger pangs a little, but their appetite for human flesh after sampling it multiple times over the last few days was now insatiable.

He felt brittle fur brush against the tips of his fingers before his wrist shattered as it smashed against the tiled floor, despite the cushioning provided by several writhing rodents. His elbow was next, snapping inwards rather than out. Bone tore through flesh and the material of his black sweater, spurting blood in a gushing arc, riling the already excited creatures into new realms of hyperactivity. His baying yowl sent a shiver through all that heard it as the rest of his body smashed down.

Agony, revulsion and horror metaphorically cocooned him in an instant, while the rats went about the business of doing it literally. Within a couple of seconds, there was not a single centimetre of his body that was not covered by the shifting blanket of dark brown fur. He felt the small animals eagerly gnawing on his freshly snapped joint. Sabre-sharp teeth tore into his cheeks and nose through the material of the ski mask, while two voracious feeders set to work on his already exposed lips, biting and ripping. He could feel his skin stretching like melted cheese until gut-wrenching pops made the elastic, blood-soaked spongy flesh twang back into position.

He closed his eyes tight, all of a sudden finding religion, praying that the multitude of creatures did not shift their attention towards the windows of his soul. All he could breathe was stink. All he could hear was the sound of his own flesh being torn, plucked, grasped and wrenched from his bones. All he could taste was blood and bile in the back of his throat, and all he could feel was torturous suffering.

His sight was the last of his senses he could protect, and he clenched his lids together tighter than ever. But then he felt it, the thing he had dreaded. Snapping teeth sliced into the bunched skin, slashing his cornea at the same time. Then the same thing on the other eye. Tear after tear forced him to watch through a bloody filter as creatures shifted for better position, letting in tiny flashes of daylight.

He felt a sharp stab in his neck then something freezing cold. His jugular. With that and the elbow wound, it wouldn't be long now. He stopped struggling, there was no point and whatever energy he had was fast leaving him. The excited shrieks carried on, the jaws continued to snap, and for all that he tried to hear his mother's voice, his sister's voice, his daughter's voice in his head, the only sounds that rang out were the high-pitched ones heralding his own death.

64

It all happened in a matter of seconds. One moment he was there, the next he was gone. Sal had seen it all unfold. She had heard the sickening crack of bone and all the hellish sounds that followed. The stench of the pit now had a coppery scent as a red hue painted many of the brown furry bodies fighting to take a bite.

She forced her gaze from the unfolding carnage and across to Lauren who was backing away from the pot-bellied figure looming ever closer to her with his sword drawn and a twisted, thrill-seeking glimmer in his eyes that Sal could make out even from ten metres back.

The other women were still tied up in their own battles. Sal's worst fears had been realised, all six hunters had descended on them at the same time. But more important than the plan, for the time being, was all of them surviving long enough to come up with another.

The man raised his sword, puffing his chest out like a silverback gorilla. *Shit!* Sal flung the mace. It somersaulted towards its target. She knew only too well that it wasn't a kill throw. At best it would injure him, shunt him off balance; at worst it would miss entirely and Lauren would be gone. She began to sprint, immediately alerting the swordsman to her presence. The blur of movement caused his gaze to shift from the terrified young woman in front of him. He spotted the hurtling mace just in time to dive out of the way. The hunter landed heavily on the ground, and Lauren turned to flee, almost running into Sal's arms. They both sprinted to the other side of the clearing, throwing a brief glance back to watch the man struggling to his feet. Before he got all the way up, the bushes rustled and parted revealing a blood-covered banshee screaming at the top of her voice with an axe raised far above her head. "Hiiiyagh!" The blade burrowed into the swordsman's spinal column. He crashed to the earth without so much as a final cry of pain.

Charlie straightened up, her lips forming a wide smile, revealing eerily white teeth to contrast with her bloody face. "Oh man, that felt good," she said, desperately trying to catch her breath.

"Is that all of them?" Sal asked.

"Yeah," Erin said, appearing behind her tall, tattooed, slightly insane friend. "Sorry, it didn't work out the way you planned it. The last two showed up just after you got the kick in the ribs; we didn't have much of a choice."

"Not really a lot we could do. At least four of us went into this battle and four of us came out. That's more than I expected."

"What now?"

"Well, first of all, I need to get my fucking leg sorted, then we get the hell out of here," Sal replied. Lauren and Erin used belts and cut one of the hunter's sweater sleeves to form a tourniquet and bandage. It wasn't ideal, but it would have to do, and it allowed Sal to walk, albeit with a limp.

When she had tried it out with a couple of circuits of the small clearing, she and Lauren collected their respective weapons and Erin claimed her very own sword and the four of them marched away from the clearing and the cameras.

It was not long before they reached the stream. They drank, they washed, and they rested for just a moment … long enough to grasp the enormity of what they had achieved.

"Hey," Charlie said, sitting down beside Sal while Erin and Lauren sat in quiet contemplation.

"Hey," Sal replied.

"That was really ballsy what you did. I don't know if I could have done it."

"I'm pretty certain you could. I think out of all of us, you're the one who could get through this thing by yourself."

Charlie smiled. "Naa. What you did, offering yourself up as bait, staying still while that twat-rag kicked you, that requires a special kind of bravery and control. I just wanted to say to you, respect." She balled her hand into a fist and held it out in front of her.

A fist bump? Really? Sal smiled and did the same. "Thanks, Charlie. Nice work by the way. I'd hate to be up against you in a ring."

"What can I tell you? I have a passion for what I do." They sat together in a comfortable silence for a few minutes; then Sal rose to her feet.

"Well, if nobody's got a better plan, I say we follow the stream back to the bridge. We do what we initially set out to do, breaking down the fence, and then we see if we can find a way off this fucking island."

"And what if—" Lauren started.

"No what ifs, Lauren. If they send another team of hunters in, if the boat's already gone, if it fucking starts raining napalm, we'll deal with it as and when. All we can do right here, right now, is try."

65

Their senses remained on high alert as they walked along the side of the stream. It was still only morning, and the sun shone brightly, making the water glisten. Another time, another situation and they may have been able to appreciate the simplistic beauty of where they were, but all they could do was look for traps and figures lurking in the shadows.

They continued until they reached the bridge. "Which way?" Erin asked.

"Well, we've been heading east. That guy said the dock was to the east, so left or right, we break through this fence, and we keep going until land stops and the sea begins, then we look for a dock," Sal replied.

"And now we've killed them all. Now every camera feed has ended, do you honestly think the boat will still be waiting there?"

"I don't know what to think. I know that while ever we're trapped on the inside of this fence, our only options are to walk around in circles and possibly get chased down by more of those sick bastards, maybe falling into the odd trap along the way. Out there though," she said, pointing to the road and the great beyond, "there's a chance. There's a chance that we might find a way to get home."

"Sal's right." It wasn't Lauren but Charlie who spoke. "Everything she said is right. We can carry on doing things their way or we can do things our way."

They turned and followed the fence for a while until they found the wreckage of the small drone. The pine trees to their left were fully grown, each reaching a good seventy or eighty feet.

Sal stopped. "I suppose this is as good a place as any." She looked towards Charlie. "We'll take it in turns while the others keep a lookout."

"No need," Charlie replied. "I can chop down a

tree, no biggie."

Sal smiled. "Yeah, no doubt, but 'A', it's fairer if we split the work, and 'B', we don't know what the hell is facing us when we get out there. You're our best fighter, and we don't want you shagged out."

Charlie shrugged. "I suppose." She walked up to one of the tall, thick pines and looked across to the fence. "I hope this idea of yours works."

"Yeah, me too. In a little while, I guess we'll know one way or another."

Charlie raised the axe and was about to make the first cut when a loud buzzing alarm sounded some distance away. "What the fuck is that?" she asked, bringing the axe back down and walking out from the trees.

The four of them began to walk in the direction of the noise, and gradually the alarm got louder until they saw the accompanying flashing red lights. "What's going on here?" Lauren asked.

"Only one way to find out," Erin replied.

They continued along the fence line until they reached the beacons. The women stopped and glanced at each other then looked towards the gate that had slid open, allowing them to leave the fenced-in confines of the battleground.

"Do you think it's a trap?" Charlie asked.

"What isn't a trap here?" Lauren replied.

"Fair point."

Sal remained quiet and just observed. She looked at the gate that had opened; she looked at the runs, the lights, at everything. Of course it was a trap, but what kind of trap? She turned and limped across to the trees.

"Sal? Sal, what are you doing?" Lauren asked as she and the others just watched.

Sal scoured the ground for a moment then found what she was looking for. It was a branch, roughly five feet in length and just a little thinner than her arm. She headed back over to the open entrance and waved the branch up and down in the gap as if she was expecting poisoned darts to shoot out at her like in a Hollywood movie. When none did, she tentatively tapped the side of the fence with the branch—nothing. She looked towards the other women and was about to cross the threshold when she stopped suddenly and leaned over, pushing the point of the long stick hard against the ground.

"Seems firm enough," she said then took a deep breath. "Okay, here goes nothing."

66

Sal paused for several seconds after crossing the threshold, just waiting for something to happen. It was a level of hysterical paranoia she had never dreamed herself capable of. She turned back to her friends. "I think it's okay.

The other three women quickly stepped through, and then the gate slowly rolled closed. "Err … I guess this means we're being watched," Erin said, and the four of them looked all around for any signs of cameras, hunters or drones.

"I think it will be safer to assume from now on that we're being watched all the time," Sal said.

"That's a comforting thought," Erin replied.

"Which way then?" Lauren asked.

"What's that?" Erin asked.

"What's what?" Charlie replied.

"That sound. It's … music."

"Oh yeah, sure. Radio One's probably doing a roadshow round the corner."

"No, she's right," Lauren said. "I hear it too."

"Yeah," Sal added. "It's coming from that direction."

"So what do we do?" Erin asked.

"Follow it," Sal replied.

"What happened to doing things our way from now on?" Charlie asked.

"Well, considering they seem to be watching every move we make, I don't think it really matters. Just keep your wits about you."

They continued following the road, with the fence to their left and another unfenced wooded area to their right. It was the trees on that side that gained most of their attention. None of them said it, but each one felt convinced that at any second hunters would appear and a fresh nightmare would begin.

The music continued to get louder but not loud enough to drown out the squawk of the odd seagull. As they approached the brow of the hill, Sal slowed down to a halt. "What are we stopping for?" Erin asked.

The loud electronic dance music continued to boom, much closer now. Sal turned to Lauren. "You're my best friend, and whatever happens next I need you to remember."

"Why are you saying this?"

"I just need you to know, that's all." She turned towards Charlie and Erin. "If we get out of this, you guys are so coming on a night out with us in Manchester," Sal said, forcing a smile.

"Fuck that," Charlie replied. "You're coming to Liverpool for the weekend. We'll have the most epic fucking send-off for our friends and yours."

"Deal," Sal said, smiling.

"Too right it's a deal. Now let's go show these wankers who they're fucking messing with."

67

Charlie strengthened her grip around the axe and led the way. The others followed, each clutching their own weapon tightly, knowing that soon they would need them again … one way or another, for the last time.

They marched over the brow of the hill and the road sloped down steeply, revealing the tranquil, shimmering sea. Their eyes were immediately drawn to a boat, bobbing on the gentle waves in the distance.

"Fuck!" Sal said as her eyes followed the blue waters into the shore. The long wooden dock was naked, a jutting bridge to nowhere.

"So what, we're just stuck here?" Lauren asked.

"Like fuck," Charlie replied. "If I've got to cut down trees and build a boat myself, we're not going to be stuck on this fucking island one minute longer than we have to be. But right now, I want to find out which cunt thinks he can hold a fucking rave while my friends are lying back there dead."

They carried on down the hill until they reached another road to their right. They turned onto it, and the music got louder still. It was not long before the drive widened out into a parking area. There was a grand looking, white two-storey house standing at the far end. To the right of it was a helicopter pad, minus the helicopter.

"I'm guessing this is where all the special guests stay after the day's hunt," Sal shouted over the sound of the booming music.

"I really fucking hope we find some of them in there," Charlie replied.

"Yeah, I wouldn't build your hopes up."

They approached the house to see flashing coloured lights behind the thick-curtained windows. The wide double doors were open, and the music was almost deafening as they stood in the entrance.

The women looked at one another. No matter how loudly they shouted, they would not be heard over the music, so they kept their mouths shut and walked down the long hallway to the open door that flashed rainbow lights against the opposite wall. They burst through, immediately raising their weapons, ready for the onslaught, but the only thing that confronted them were banks of twirling disco lights, enormous speakers and a table with a dozen champagne bottles in the centre and ten glasses. There was a banner hanging over it saying:

TO THE VICTOR BELONG THE SPOILS

They walked up to the table. As thirsty as they were, it would be a cold day in hell before any of them drank a drop of the two-hundred-pounds-a-bottle bubbly that had been laid out for the uber-wealthy hunters and their henchmen.

Four sets of headphones sat in front of the champagne bottles. The women placed them on, blocking the sound of much of the music. The lights suddenly stopped flashing, the booming sounds muted further, and a huge TV screen lit up on the wall. There was a middle-aged, dark-haired man with almost black eyes sitting in a luxurious leather armchair, looking straight towards the camera. He wore a thin smile on his face, and for a moment, he said nothing, he just stared, sending goose bumps running up and down his audience's arms.

"I learnt a long time ago that with enough money you can do anything you want," he began. "You can buy all things, and you can even buy people. Not all people but some. You four are true gladiators. It has been most enjoyable watching you. In sixteen years, we have never had contestants who have beaten the system the way you have. So—" he raised a glass of champagne "—congratulations, I drink to you, one and all. Thank you for putting a smile on my face." He tilted the glass and glugged its contents, placing it down carefully before crossing his hands in his lap once more.

Charlie took a step towards the screen, "Thanks, that's really sweet, now could you do us all a favour, and fuck off and die?"

The man stared for a few seconds then broke out into a much wider smile. "Despite what you may think, I am a man of honour."

"Oh yeah. It's really honourable to kidnap young women then have a bunch of sick fucking psychos hunt them down so you can line your pockets. Fuck me, you must be the most honourable man in the world to let all that happen," Charlie replied.

He ignored the comments and continued. "Because of your bravery and your resolve, I want to give you all a chance. This can stop, right here, right now. You will never be able to return home, but you can come and work for me. I will pay you well. You will live good lives. Or the game will continue. I will give you a moment to thi—"

Charlie's axe destroyed the screen in one smash. It fell to the ground in a fountain of sparks and flames. She watched it with a self-satisfied smile as it hit the floor then turned around to the others and pulled the headphones from her ears. They all did the same.

The music was still playing, but it was much quieter than it had been when they'd first walked in. "Come on. Let's get the fuck out of here," Charlie said, heading towards the door.

"Wait a minute," Sal replied.

"Wait for what?"

"What he said, the thing about the game continuing. That probably means there's going to be another team of hunters out there waiting for us."

"Fucking bring it on," Charlie replied, clutching her axe in both hands. "I've had enough of this shit."

She started towards the door again but suddenly loud metallic clunking thuds sounded from all over the house, and the disco lights resumed. Sal ran to the window and threw the thick curtains open. A solid metal shield had been lowered, covering the entire opening, blocking the entry of any daylight. She banged against it with her fist. "You'd need a fucking tank to get through that."

Lauren ran out of the room and down the hallway. "The front door's the same. It's blocked." She turned to look at the staircase. "Shit, Sal, the stairs are blocked too." She ran back into the room with fresh panic on her face.

"So what the fuck's all this about?" Charlie asked.

"I've no idea, but something tells me that we're about to find out," Sal replied.

The lights continued to flash, but the music went into a fast fade. "What's that sound?" Lauren asked.

"It's just the hiss of the speakers," Erin replied.

"No. It sounds like … scratching."

All four of them listened more carefully, and as their eardrums adjusted to no longer hearing pounding drum and bass riffs, one by one they realised what the sound was.

"Oh fuck, no!" Charlie said.

"Quick," Sal said, storming out of the room. The others followed. She reached into her pocket, bringing out her key fob with the small torch attached. She flicked it on as they ran down the dark corridor. They followed the hallway to the right, and Sal came to a crashing stop as the others piled into her. Another solid metal barrier blocked the way. The scratching sounds could be heard out here too, and the slightly thinner walls allowed the terrifying hungry squeals of an unimaginable number of rats to drift through.

"Oh no," Erin said.

They reluctantly headed back to the only room they had access to. The lights still flashed, and now the scratching noise was louder than ever.

"It sounds like they're in the walls, behind the skirting boards, under the floor, everywhere," Erin said in a shaky voice.

The four of them walked into the middle of the large reception room and stood back to back. In such close proximity, they could smell one another's B. O. as more sweat than ever headed over their skin, but all of them knew they were about to smell something much worse.

69

It sounded like a door being unlocked … that's what it sounded like, but it wasn't that at all. Every skirting board fell forward, and thousands of screeching, hissing, evil-smelling rodents burst into the room like a vomitous tidal wave.

Sal heard Lauren begin to cry; then she started too. There was no point in pretending to be strong anymore. It was a rigged game. It had always been a rigged game. She dropped her weapon on the floor and turned, pulling Lauren around to face her. They squeezed each other, and Sal placed her hand around the back of Lauren's head. "We're not here. We're not here, darling, we're in that little taverna in Zakynthos where the waiters were constantly chatting us up and getting us drinks on the house. We're on that pedalo where we went so far out to see the turtles that we were scared we couldn't make it back to land. We're—"

"Aaarrrggghhh!" Charlie began stamping and chopping with her axe, refusing to give up, but it was futile.

Erin dropped to her knees, letting out a chilling shriek as a dozen creatures pounced all at once.

Sal continued to hold Lauren tight, even when she felt clawing feet racing up her body. "We're not here, darling … we're not here." They both cried together, feeling each other's tears against their skin. "Remember that rock, that rock at the top of that cliff where we looked out over the Mediterranean—" Sal felt teeth begin to gnash and bite the bloody wound on her side, but she carried on. "—and we said we'd be best friends until the day we died. Well, we were. We were, darling."

Neither spoke after that, they just held each other and carried on crying until the weight of the animals on them and the bites to their muscles and tendons became too much. They collapsed to the ground. The screams and cries of pain went unheard to everyone but Charlie who continued to battle and kick and grunt and chop, but eventually she succumbed too.

She collapsed to her knees, her entire body covered in writhing, excited, squealing rodents. She had always had a high threshold for pain, but as she felt the life literally bleeding out of her, she let out one last angry yowl.

***

The betting had stopped the moment the rats flooded into the room. Tattoo girl had been the favourite to be the last woman standing by far, so Sarafian had taken a hit on the final bet of the tournament, but it was a drop in the ocean. He had fixed a limit on this one, and what he paid out was nothing compared to what he had made.

He sat there a moment longer looking at the screens. Hayk and Lilit whispered excitedly to each other as they broke down the stage betting and frantically tapped away on calculators. They didn't understand. The money … there was always and would always be plenty of money, but today had been something different.

Today, Sarafian had found himself rooting for those girls. He knew what their answer would be to his offer, and, realistically, he could never have trusted them anyway, so he would have ended up killing them, but not like this. They deserved more than just being another game for the uber-wealthy to have a flutter on, they deserved respect.

He climbed to his feet and lit another cigarette. "I'm going to my hotel," he said, heading out of the room.

"Papa, don't you want to hear the final figures? We are nearly done," Lilit said.

"No," he replied, turning to look at her. "Remember, Avet and Grigor will be here within the hour to begin sanitisation, so make sure you are gone by then."

"Yes, Papa," they replied simultaneously before returning to their calculations.

Sarafian left the darkened room and headed out of the office suite into the abandoned warehouse that one of his shell companies owned. Maybe he was getting too old for all of this, becoming too sentimental. He stopped suddenly as a giant black rat ran across the floor in front of him. A shiver ran down his spine, and a freeze-frame image of those two girls holding each other tightly flashed into his brain. To have a friend like that, to have a friend to die with, to share death with … that would be something.

A tear of regret appeared in the corner of his eye. "I'm sorry," he whispered before heading out to the waiting car. He gave one final look back to the dilapidated warehouse complex as he was chauffeured away. It was not long before his mobile phone buzzed, snapping him from his melancholy thoughts; it was a text message.

June 15–20 - New Zealand - reservations confirmed - arrangements in place.

Sarafian let out a sad sigh. *And so it begins again.*

The End

A NOTE FROM THE AUTHOR

I really hope you enjoyed this book and would be very grateful if you took a minute to leave a review on Amazon and Goodreads.

If you would like to stay informed about what I'm doing, including current writing projects, and all the latest news and release information; these are the places to go:

Join the fan club on Facebook
https://www.facebook.com/groups/127693634504226

Like the Christopher Artinian author page
https://www.facebook.com/safehaventrilogy/

Buy exclusive and signed books and merchandise, subscribe to the newsletter and follow the blog:

https://www.christopherartinian.com/

Follow me on Twitter
https://twitter.com/Christo71635959

Follow me on Youtube:
https://www.youtube.com/channel/UCfJymx31Vvztt B_Q-x5otYg

Follow me on Amazon
https://amzn.to/2I1llU6

Follow me on Goodreads
https://bit.ly/2P7iDzX

Other books by Christopher Artinian:

Safe Haven: Rise of the RAMs
Safe Haven: Realm of the Raiders
Safe Haven: Reap of the Righteous
Safe Haven: Ice
Safe Haven: Vengeance
Safe Haven: Is This the End of Everything?
Before Safe Haven: Lucy
Before Safe Haven: Alex
Before Safe Haven: Mike
Before Safe Haven: Jules
The End of Everything: Book 1
The End of Everything: Book 2
The End of Everything: Book 3

The End of Everything: Book 4

The End of Everything: Book 5

The End of Everything: Book 6

The End of Everything: Book 7

Anthologies featuring short stories by Christopher Artinian

Undead Worlds: A Reanimated Writers Anthology

Featuring: Before Safe Haven: Losing the Battle by Christopher Artinian

Tales from Zombie Road: The Long-Haul Anthology

Featuring: Condemned by Christopher Artinian

Treasured Chests: A Zombie Anthology for Breast Cancer Care

Featuring: Last Light by Christopher Artinian

Trick or Treat Thrillers (Best Paranormal 2018)

Featuring: The Akkadian Vessel.

CHRISTOPHER ARTINIAN

Christopher Artinian was born and raised in Leeds, West Yorkshire. Wanting to escape life in a big city and concentrate more on working to live than living to work, he and his family moved to the Outer Hebrides in the north-west of Scotland in 2004, where he now works as a full-time author.

Chris is a huge music fan, a cinephile, an avid reader and a supporter of Yorkshire county cricket club. When he's not sat in front of his laptop living out his next post-apocalyptic/dystopian/horror adventure, he will be passionately immersed in one of his other interests.

Printed in Great Britain
by Amazon